KISSING TOLSTOY

DEAR PROFESSOR SERIES #1

PENNY REID

KISSING TOLSTOY

BY PENNY REID

http://pennyreid.ninja/newsletter
Caped Publishing

Caped Publishing
Made in the United States of America
November 2017
PRINT EDITION
ISBN-13: 978-1-942874-36-2

hat do I have to lose?

All I needed to do was email the guy, set up the date, pray he was even a fifth as amazing as Emily said he was, and show up. That's it.

I am such a Scaredy McFrightenedton . . .

Staring at the blinking cursor on my screen, I eyed the "x" in the upper right-hand corner. I could just close the window, navigate to the start menu, select *shut down,* and watch my computer screen fade to black.

One year. Twelve months. Just a week shy of three hundred sixty-five days.

Somewhere in the rebellious recesses of my mind, an annoying little voice (sounding suspiciously like my own) reminded me that nearly twelve months had passed since my last date. Since my boyfriend had broken up with me via text message, completely out of the blue, on Valentine's Day.

On the scale of awful, it rated pretty high. This was because the text he'd sent was a picture of him kissing another girl. I was completely blindsided. One minute we were solid, and the next he was in the running for the world's biggest-bag-of-dicks trophy.

In other words, my ex was the John Willoughby to my Marianne Dashwood, if John Willoughby had quoted Pokémon and anime instead of Shakespearean sonnets. And Marianne had liked him mostly for his skills as a trivia night partner and cheerful acceptance of her jigsaw puzzle habit.

Even though my heart hadn't been broken, it had been bruised. Afterward, I had difficulty trusting my own judgment. He'd seemed *so nice*. Nerdy nice. My kind of nice.

And though I hadn't run recklessly into a rainstorm and nearly died of pneumonia, I'd sworn off romantic relationships with non-fictional characters (i.e. other real humans) for the remainder of my life. At the time, it felt like an easy promise to keep.

But now, after almost twelve months and Valentine's Day looming, I felt restless, surprisingly ready to throw my hat in the ring again. Get my groove on. I might even be persuaded to watch Netflix and chill.

And yet, I wasn't so sure.

What do you have to lose?

The thought troubled me and I debated the nature of loss, realizing—sans the possibility that this guy Emily wanted to set me up with was literally a serial killer—all I had to lose was time. Time I would most likely otherwise spend watching *A Room with a View* and rewinding the scene on the hill over and over and over and over.

The one where Julian Sands grabs Helena Bonham Carter with his big man-hands, holding her around the waist and sliding his—I imagined—cool fingers over her cheek, then pulling her to him with expectation. And as their lips meet for the first time, amidst the sea of golden barley, the kiss explodes with passion.

And there it was.

The possibility of passion, and maybe even the possibility of *real* heartbreak, feelings for a person beyond the safety of my comfort zone, the risk of actually wanting to run recklessly into a rainstorm, had me internally monologue a pep talk.

Screw fear of the unknown! Carpe Diem! Seize the fucking day!

I nodded, and then began typing.

Hi Lucas,

You don't know me . . . and I don't know how to do this. But rest assured, the most terrible and terrifying thing has already been written (the most terrible thing being the word "hi", because—in this circumstance—it is also the bravest).

Now that my awkward reference to Anna Karenina has been made, let me start again:

Hi Lucas,

You don't know me. Our mutual friend (Emily Von) gave me your email address. Emily has told me many times that she thinks we would be perfect for each other, that it'll be "love at first sight."

Even though I'm a romantic, I don't believe in love at first sight; the concept strikes me as frivolous and convenient. As Tolstoy said, "It is amazing how complete is the delusion that beauty is goodness."

But I digress.

If you're interested in meeting up, please come to Jake Peterson's Microbrewery on Fifth and Pine this Saturday at 6 p.m. (Valentine's Day). I'll be the one in leather pants.

Looking forward to it, Anna I. Harris

PS Don't ask what the "I" stands for because I won't tell you.

On a rush of adrenaline, I typed the message and the email address from the card Emily had given me, and hit send. And then I reveled in my courage and guts and ability to seize the moment, taking wide steps around my apartment with my head held high. I smiled at my reflection and the inspiration of meeting at the microbrewery, most likely brought on by the picturesque barley field of Lucy and George's first kiss.

I also patted myself on the back—literally, in front of the mirror—for having the tits to schedule the date for V-day.

I spent a full minute congratulating myself, dwelling on my amazingness, before anxiety hit me like a punch in the throat.

What have I done?

* * *

Nervous wreck? Basket case? How about deer caught in headlights?

Oh yeah, all those idioms and more.

What am I doing here? What are you doing?

I glanced down at my outfit—leather pants. Leather-fracking-pants. Leather pants purchased from a thrift store. I was in someone else's leather pants.

As a college student responsible for my own bills, I couldn't afford brand-new leather pants. But I was also a cosplay aficionado, and therefore owned leather pants.

You know, for costumes.

My part-time job working at the Natural History Muse-um's swanky restaurant as a server allowed me to maintain the ostentatious lifestyle to which I'd become accustomed: a 1992 Honda Civic with no original parts, tragic romance novels, early edition—and maybe a little moldy—fiction classics, boxes of wine, ramen noodles, and thrift store finds for my cosplay costumes. My modest student loans helped cover school costs beyond my academic scholarships; I was determined to graduate with as little debt as possible.

Besides, the best things in life can all be found at thrift stores. Just ask my collection of David Bowie faces on *Labyrinth*-themed coffee mugs.

But back to now, because right now, I was certifiable. I needed to find the nearest sane person and sign over my rights to decision making, or at least give them my laptop. Might as well throw in my passcode to the computer lab on campus.

Severely apprehensive, I glanced around the microbrewery and rehearsed for the seventh time all the excuses I could give to leave early when he eventually showed up . . . if he showed up.

It was already five minutes after 6:00 p.m.

He is not coming. You are a moron in a stranger's leather pants, and he is not coming because you are a moron. This is what you get for reading all those books.

I tucked my hair—worn in a halo of curls—nervously behind my ear and glanced at my watch again, unable to miss the cleavage beneath the purple V-neck I'd decided to wear.

I'd justified it earlier by reminding myself that today was laundry day. What I didn't want to think about was showing up in leather pants and my green granny sweater, the only other clean item in my closet.

Chewing on my lip, I shifted in my seat. The waiter looked my way and our eyes met. His gaze flickered to my chest. He smiled shortly. He turned and attended to another table. The knot in the pit of my stomach twisted.

Oh great, now Mr. I-am-married-waiter-guy feels sorry for Ms. Ridiculous-in-leather-pants. I rolled my eyes, reminding myself that no one looks good in leather pants, not in real life.

Then, I looked up and saw leather pants.

Leather pants, leather boots, leather jacket, leather motor-cycle gloves, and blue eyes. The bluest eyes I'd ever seen. As mesmerizing as his eyes were, I couldn't help but notice the rest of him. Thick muscular thighs, broad muscular chest and arms, square-cut jaw, and blond spiked hair. For a moment, I thought he was *him*. My blind date.

However, a split second later, as I attempted to swallow my lust, I'd convinced myself he was not *him*.

Yes, he had blond hair like Emily had described. Yes, he had blue eyes. Yes, he was tall. But, Lucas had also been described as "artsy." This man sure as hell wasn't artsy. Sure, his body was a work of art, his movements were artful, but I'd never describe him as "artsy."

Not-artsy was combing the brewery, turning his head this way and that as though searching for someone. I hadn't had time to compose myself when his eyes locked with mine, and then it was impossible to tear my gaze away.

He smirked.

I swallowed.

He walked toward me.

I swallowed again.

He halted at my table, but I was out of saliva and my mouth felt cottony and useless.

He dipped his head as though waiting for me to speak. Finally, raising his eyebrows, he asked, "Anna I. Harris?"

The sound of my name coming from his mouth broke me from the trance.

I stood inelegantly, causing the chair to scrape noisily on the wood floor, and extended my hand. "Yes, um—yes! I'm Anna, you must be—"

He cut me off, moving a chair closer to mine and said, "Sit."

And I did. My face flushed with embarrassment. *What am I? A dog? Sit. Bark. Roll over.* My face flushed again, this time from unbidden images of me rolling over with him on top.

Whoa!

He was watching me, his elbow resting carelessly on the table, and I burned brighter under his scrutiny. Realizing I could clear my throat, I did.

"So, um, thanks for coming." I glanced up, meeting his scrutiny.

He examined me with obvious interest before clearing his throat. "Tell me about yourself."

"Oh. Okay." I sat straighter in my seat. "Uh, I'm a third year electrical engineering major. I work at the Natural History Museum as a server in the restaurant, but I have an internship lined up for next fall at—"

"This isn't a job interview." He was smiling, and it continued to grow by the slowest of degrees until his eyes ignited and sparkled; at least to me they appeared to be sparkling. "Tell me about you. Where did you grow up?"

"A few hours outside of Chicago. And you?"

"Do you have any siblings?"

"No. But I have two cousins I'm very close to. They're a few years older, but my aunt watched me while my dad worked, so they felt like older siblings."

"What do they do?"

"Um, Marie is a journalist in Chicago, and Abram," I had to pause, because my cousin Abram was incorrigible, but also awesome. "He's a musician in New York. Do you have any siblings?"

"One sister, older, Dominika. She's . . ." He gave me a look that communicated both exasperation and affection. "She's a handful. What about your parents? How did they meet?"

"Uh, let's see." I grinned at him, unable to help myself. Being near him felt electrifying, exciting. Or he was magnetic. Or his obvious interest in me made me feel magnetized toward him. Something like that. "My parents were nurses. They met in Nigeria—where my mother was from—when my father worked for Doctors Without Borders in the late nineteen eighties."

"Was from?" He tilted his head to the side just slightly, frowning.

"Yes." I nodded, feeling myself grow rigid. "My mother died when I was little."

His expression noticeably softened, and—as though I'd caught him off guard—he blurted, "My mother died when I was eight."

At his admission, my breath caught. Jeez. *What were the chances?*

I wanted to cover his gloved hand with mine, offer comfort. I knew it still hurt to think about, let alone discuss. But I stayed my fingers and instead leaned forward.

"Really?"

He nodded, rubbing his bottom lip with his forefinger, his stare thoughtful. "What brought you to New England?" A hint of what sounded like suspicion entered his voice.

"College. I thought about going to the University of Chicago, or maybe Michigan, but I wanted a change." I knew

I needed new experiences, new people, new places. I needed to force myself to be adventurous before life became a predictable series of days, each an exercise in responsible adulthood.

Silence fell between us as my gaze flickered over Lucas. The silence wasn't awkward, and it wasn't heavy. It just was. It struck me that today—this moment—was the most adventurous I'd been since leaving home. And that left me wondering if this guy was for real.

His body inclined forward and he studied me studying him. "Am I not what you expected?" he asked quietly, like the question was a secret between us.

My eyes widened and I automatically shook my head. "No, of course I—" I looked away, searching for a plausible and polite half-truth that wouldn't have me admitting he was *better* than I'd expected. Ultimately, I decided the best way to keep things from getting weird was to admit as little as possible.

So I lifted my eyes again. "Well, actually, yes. You are not what I expected."

He raised his eyebrows and scooted his chair closer. "How so?"

I smiled, feeling more at ease and more anxious at the same time. "Well, Emily said you were artsy and somehow . . ." I gestured to him with my hand, unable to finish my sentence.

His expression unreadable, he responded flatly, "I'm not artsy."

I couldn't help it, I laughed. His smile returned, small but genuine, and so did the sparkle in his eyes. This time it felt sharper, more purposeful.

Indicating with his chin to my lower half, he said, "Nice pants."

My laughter faded. I tucked a curl behind my ear and narrowed my eyes. "Yeah, well, yours aren't bad either. Where do you shop? The Leather Warehouse?"

Leaning back in his chair, he smirked and pulled off the leather jacket and gloves, like he'd just made up his mind to stay awhile. Removing his jacket revealed a charcoal-gray T-shirt that proved my suspicions about his chest right. Realizing I was staring, I forced myself to look away. "So, um, Emily said—"

Glancing to the side and exhaling, he shook his head. "Look, I need to tell you something."

Oh God. He's married. He's a eunuch. He's gay. He hates my leather pants.

I tried not to let my panic show as he stared at me. Making certain I was paying attention, he leaned in close. "I'm not who you think I am."

My eyebrows pulled low, evidence of my confusion.

He continued, "I think you sent me that email by accident. I don't know anyone named Emily. And no one tried to set me up with an Anna."

My jaw dropped in despair and a rush of intense embarrassment seized my insides. "Oh my God." I stood, reached for my bag, and backed away from the table.

Clearly anticipating my movements, the stranger grabbed my hand. This didn't deter me from intermittently muttering curses and apologies.

"I'm so sorry, this is not, I mean, I'm sorry you came all the way to—I don't know what the hell I was—you are definitely not—and I'm not—"

"Listen," he stood and moved his grip from my hand to my elbow, "wait."

I raised my eyes to his, shaking my head. "Why did you even come?"

He took a step forward, dwarfing me. His hand felt strong and sure—I noticed this without wanting to—and he shifted it to my waist, holding me still and sending heat to my stomach.

Dipping his head to the side and leaning close, he whispered, "I wanted to know what the 'I' stood for."

PART 2

*** ANNA ***

"So, did you tell him? What the 'I' stands for?" Emily waved her celery stick through the air, her eager eyes betraying how completely absorbed she'd been in my telling of the story.

"What? No!" I shook my head, glaring at my friend. She'd lost her damn mind. "Of course not."

She sighed; it sounded like a deflating tire. "Why *of course not*?"

I struggled for a minute to explain, then finally settled on, "Because he was in leather pants."

"So were you." Emily hopped onto the counter adjacent to where I was cooking tomato sauce for dinner.

"Yes, but I don't normally wear leather pants. He looked like he always wore leather pants. Like maybe he showered in them."

Emily wrinkled her nose at this. "Gross."

"No, no. He wasn't dirty, what I mean is: he looked really good in the pants. He looked like leather pants were his thing."

My friend crunched on the celery stick she'd been waving

around earlier. "Okay, you've completely lost me. You didn't give this hot guy your middle name—or your number—because he looks good in leather pants?"

"Unnaturally good. And he wore leather gloves. And a leather jacket. And he left on a motorcycle." I thought for a moment, stirring the red sauce and becoming mildly flushed once again as I recalled him speeding away while straddling the motorcycle. He didn't know I'd been watching him.

After he'd asked me for my middle name, my brain failed me and I was crushed by a wave of embarrassment. I couldn't physically form words. I'd just told a complete stranger about my parents, my childhood, my family, my mother.

I felt ill.

I'd handed over significant and exceptionally personal details about my past. I'd blamed this uncharacteristic willingness to share on my assumption that he was friends with Emily, and therefore trustworthy.

But if I was honest with myself, it was really because of his sparkly eyes. The memory of my ex was too fresh. I still couldn't trust my own judgment—definitely not where guys were concerned—so I gave him a panicked smile, mumbled something mostly incomprehensible about going to the bathroom, and bolted out the back door of the restaurant.

I hid in my car, unable to leave but too mortified to stay.

He'd strolled out twenty minutes later, glanced around the parking lot, looking like a perfect mixture of a young Paul Newman and Chris Hemsworth. I'd ducked, only peeking over my dashboard when I heard the rumble of a motorcycle. His back was to me, providing a nice view of his long legs and leather-clad torso. Straddling the bike, he kicked up his stand and drove off into the sunset like a troubled hero from one of those movies I watched too much—*Rebel Without a Cause* or *On the Waterfront*.

I sighed at the memory and reminded myself out loud, "He was a complete stranger."

"So?"

"So, I rely on you to know my type. He was definitely not my type."

"Let me ask you this." Emily nudged my knee with her foot. "Did he have a penis?"

I felt my face pinch and draw to a point as I inspected Emily's wide, green eyes. "I didn't see it if that's what you're asking." *Cue sad trombone.*

"No. I'm asking you to guess. Did the sexy guy in leather, who I'm assuming you haven't stopped fixating on for the last three days—*don't deny it!*—do you think he has a penis?"

I squirmed where I stood and felt my face do odd things. Inexplicably, I was sweating. Maybe not so inexplicably, because I was now thinking about the hot stranger's third leg.

"I'll take your weird dance as a yes. Furthermore," Emily's next bite rang with a triumphant crunch and she spoke around the piece of celery, "I maintain his leather-clad assets plus the existence of his penis makes him the right type for every heterosexual woman. Admit it, he was universal-hot-guy dating material and you let him slip through your leather gloves."

I snorted inelegantly. Then, because it was just Emily and me, I did the huff-snort-laugh of disbelief. "Uh, I'd like to think I require more than just a beefcake with a frequent shopper's card to the leather warehouse."

"You said he was nice."

She had me there.

I added more oregano to the sauce, but said nothing.

She nudged my knee again with her foot, smiling a smug smile as she sing-songed, "Admit it. He was nice. And hot. And he could have been smart and funny, but you'll never know. You left, because you freaked out like a dork."

"Fine. Fine, I freaked out like a dork! You would've too. I'm telling you, just looking at him, he wasn't the kind of guy girls like us date."

"Girls like us? You mean smart, funny, incredibly beautiful and talented girls?"

I gave her a reluctant smile, because we were normal girls.

Smart and funny? Yeah. Sure.

Incredibly beautiful and talented? Hard to say, mostly because I don't think women who are beautiful by societal standards usually realize they're beautiful, not really. I've never met a person who had an accurate grasp of their own physical beauty (or lack thereof).

Therefore, hard to say.

Was I beautiful? I didn't think so.

Better just not to dwell on it.

"Nice girls," I clarified. "We're nice girls. That's what I meant."

She gave me a face so I held up my saucy wooden spoon. "Don't give me that face. We are nice girls. This guy, he was nice, but he wasn't *nice*."

"Look at you. You're a Judging Jessica. Now who isn't being nice?"

"That's not what I mean. I'm not being judgmental. I'm just saying, I would've bored him. I'm boring-nice. I'm not riding-a-motorcycle nice, or wearing-leather-pants-frequently nice, or going-to-the-gym-for-fun nice, or going-to-clubs-and-sexy-dancing nice."

"Unless it's eighties night. We go to clubs on eighties night."

I reduced the heat of the sauce and turned my attention to

the boiling pot of spaghetti. "See? That just proves my point. We like to dance to *eighties* music, where it's acceptable to do the robot and other various and sundry dorky dances."

Emily frowned. "So what? That's not boring. That's awesome."

"Yes. To us and *our kind,* that's awesome. To Leather-pants, that's boring and lame. He probably goes to clubs and sexes up strangers against walls. He looked like that kind of guy, like he could. Like that's what he does on Tuesdays."

Now it was Emily's turn to give me a pinched look. "And you know this how?"

I shrugged, pulling a string of spaghetti from the pot and testing its mushiness. "These are truths universally acknowl-edged. Men who ride motorcycles, who wear leather like a second skin, and look hot doing it, they don't date ladies who idolize Tolstoy. Tuesday night is trivia night for me, unless I have a new jigsaw puzzle I'm excited about or I'm in my tragic novel reading cave."

"Again, awesome. Who doesn't like trivia night and jigsaw puzzles?"

"Hot men who spend their Tuesdays having sex with hot women."

"But he could do both. Hot sex, then trivia."

I huffed, because I knew she was playing devil's advocate without being serious. Time for her to face facts.

"Be honest with yourself, Em. What would you have done if you'd been in my place?" Emily opened her mouth as though to argue, but I gave her a hard look and challenged, "Be serious."

She frowned as she considered my words, her shoulders slumping. I drained the spaghetti, a ball of irritation and rest-lessness forming in my stomach the longer she stayed mute. Part of me hoped she'd continue to tell me I was wrong. Tell me I was being narrow-minded, that she would have stayed and shared a drink, swapped numbers, gone on a motorcycle ride.

But she didn't.

After several minutes, Emily hopped down from the counter and grabbed plates from the cabinet, asking, "You have the motorcycle guy's email still? Has he tried to contact you?"

"Nope. He didn't email me back. And I deleted the email."

She nodded distractedly. "I guess I would've done the same as you, unless he emailed me. If he'd emailed me after the fact, then I would reevaluate."

"Reevaluate?"

Ignoring my question, she changed the subject. "Do you want Lucas's number? Like I said, he's artsy, and definitely our kind of nice."

"Sure. Yes. Thank you." I tried to give her a smile.

And she tried to give me one in return.

***

I did call Lucas Kraft.

And he was definitely my kind of nice.

We played Pokémon Go together and assembled a puzzle for our first date.

It was good times.

But then we kissed.

That was not good times. He wasn't a good kisser. Or maybe we weren't good at kissing each other.

He didn't call me. I didn't call him. I got busy. I forgot about him. In fact, I forgot about dating a real life man. I started reading a really good book by a new-to-me author who wrote alternate reality versions of Brontë novels and spent the next few weeks immersed in her backlist. I dated her fictional heroes instead in an unapologetic phase of serial book-boyfriend polygamy.

Presently, two months later and mid-phone conversation with Emily regarding summer plans, I discovered Lucas had started dating a tattoo artist named Starla with three tongue piercings. They were moving in together after knowing each other for two weeks.

"Anna? Anna, are you still there?"

I nodded, frowning blindly at the Russian Literature class syllabus tucked into the front of my folder. "Yes. I'm still here."

"Are you . . . okay?"

I nodded tightly, not understanding why she sounded so muffled or why my heart thudded so loudly between my ears.

"I thought you didn't hit it off?"

I shook my head, completely perplexed by how hard I was taking artsy Lucas's alteration in love-life luck.

I should have called him. Then maybe I would be moving into an apartment with my new boyfriend.

What?

No. No, you shouldn't have called him. He was boring and kissed like a hamster.

I had to physically shake myself to break from my oddball crisis.

What is wrong with you?

"Excuse me?"

Too late I realized I'd spoken *What is wrong with you?* aloud. "Sorry, nothing. No. I'm good. I'm fine. That's great for Lucas and his lady friend. That's really great."

But it wasn't great.

How come lazy-tongued Lucas gets a Starla? Shouldn't he get a Suzie or a Suanne? Or an Anna? A *nice,* normal-named woman who matched his type of nice?

Not a tri-pierced Starla!

She probably looks really good in leather pants.

"Well, anyway." I heard Emily start the engine of her car. "I can't believe you're taking classes over your senior summer, and Russian Literature? Gag!"

"Don't *gag* at me. You know I love all things needlessly angsty and dramatic. Who dressed up like Rodion Raskolnikov last year for Halloween and won all the awards? Me."

"You won one contest. One. And it was for 'Most Awesome Costume No One Can Identify.'"

"It doesn't matter, I still won."

"Shouldn't you be trying to enjoy your last summer before becoming a real adult?" Emily made no attempt to disguise her disgust for my summer plans.

"You mean binge-watching Netflix and picking up extra shifts at the museum?"

"Yes. Exactly."

"No. I've been trying to get into this class for two years and it's always full. This is my last chance."

"That's because the professor is supposed to be a hottie."

"Of course he is. Professor Kroft discusses classical Russian literature for a living. If that author guy taught a course in classical Russian literature, that actress lady would leave her dancer husband for him."

"You mean Natalie Portman?"

"Who? No. The other one. Maybe it was a supermodel and he plays football. There are too many famous people. How am I supposed to keep them all straight?"

She chuckled. "You're hopeless."

"Point is," I lowered my voice to a whisper as I entered the lecture hall, "being a world-class expert in classical Russian literature would make anyone hot."

Emily snorted, but tried to hide it with a cough. "Right.

Well, anyway. I'll leave you to it. Don't forget, trivia night tomorrow. And it's the semi-finals. We need your brain for the book questions. And the periodic table questions. And—"

"Ah. Yes." I scanned the auditorium, irritated that all the seats toward the front were already taken. The closest I could get to the lecture stand was fourteen rows back. The place was packed. "I'll be there."

"Good. Talk later. Enjoy your angst."

"I will. It will feed my dark, dark soul. Bye." I clicked off, careful to turn my phone all the way off before slipping it in my bag. If three years of college had taught me anything, it was that professors hated being interrupted—by anything, but especially cell phones.

I spent the next several minutes arranging my laptop on the table in front of me, organizing my pens, the class syllabus, notepad, and the two paperback novels I'd already re-read (and highlighted, and flagged) as a prerequisite for the class. Once everything was organized to my liking, I allowed myself to look around.

The room was buzzing with excitement, which made my heart do a flip. I was obviously with my people. I was with the lovers of Dostoyevsky and Chekhov.

Who knows? I might even find my kind of nice here.

The last of my freak-out vibes from earlier dissipated. I didn't need Lucas and his hamster kisses. I decided my peculiar reaction must've been temporary insanity. So what if I didn't have a boyfriend? So what if I never had one? Loneliness and self-sacrificing despair were staples of all great classic novels. Maybe true happiness was embracing the tragedy of a solitary existence.

That sounded nice.

Cats and coffee and wretchedness. Maybe even a little typhoid and tuberculosis thrown in for maximum affect.

I couldn't wait for the lecture to begin.

"Hiya, I'm Taylor."

I turned to my left, encountering a bright-eyed brunette with her hand outstretched. I accepted her handshake.

"I'm Anna."

"Good to meet you. I can't believe I got into this class." She leaned forward as she said this last part. "I've been trying for two semesters, but it's always full."

"I know," I enthusiastically agreed. "I love that it's so popular. Which of the prerequisites did you read?"

She blinked at me. "What?"

"The prerequisites? Which did you read? I've already read *Crime and Punishment* one hundred times, so I opted for Pushkin's *Eugene Onegin*, which I've read before, but not recently."

I stopped talking because Taylor was giving me a blank stare. Confused, I glanced behind me. Finding nothing amiss, I turned to her again.

"Is there something wrong?"

She shook her head, issuing me a look that made me feel as though I might have sprouted antlers. "No. It's just, I can't believe you've already read these books. And on purpose. And more than once."

Her response startled me, but before I could interrogate her further, a hush fell over the lecture hall. Soon the only sound in the large room was leather soles on the wood floor as I craned my neck to get a peek at our professor.

"Holy cow," Taylor exclaimed under her breath, also twisting her neck and dipping her head to the side. "That man can wear a suit."

I didn't argue, because she was right. Professor Kroft did look good in a suit. At least, his backside looked good in a suit. He'd entered through a side door and was currently standing with his back to us. The professor was organizing paper printouts and books on the long table at the front.

And then he turned.

And I almost fell out of my chair.

"This course is entitled *Classics of Russian Literature*, and I am your professor, Luca Kroft." He paused, the bluest eyes I'd ever seen dispassionately surveyed the inhabitants of the first few rows.

I knew they were the bluest eyes I'd ever seen because I'd been up close and personal with them once before.

On Valentine's Day.

At Jake Peterson's Microbrewery on Fifth and Pine.

Except, instead of a suit, he'd been wearing leather pants.

PART 3

** ANNA **

"*R*ussian literature, as you're likely aware, probes into the complexities and depths of the human soul. And since we are dealing with matters of the soul, I will tolerate no disruptions." Professor Kroft's entirely too attractive voice was the only sound in the room. "Let me be clear before we begin. If you are late, you will be locked out. If you leave, you will be locked out. The doors, which are now closed, are locked."

He held us captivated with his arresting gaze as it scanned the hall, peering at all of us and none of us at once.

I ducked, my heart in my throat, my face flushed.

Oh my God.

It's him.

It's Mr. Leather-warehouse.

I forced myself to breathe, not meeting Taylor's gaze as she inspected me. My hands were shaking. I gripped the desk.

What is wrong with me?

It was the shock. That's what it was. That's why I was behaving like a loon. Again. The temporary insanity had returned. I was overreacting. I just needed to . . . *leave.*

Leave!

But I couldn't, not yet. He was speaking. If I left then I'd draw attention to myself.

Stay until the end of class, then leave!

Yes. Much better plan.

And act normal.

Impossible.

"What?" Taylor whispered at my side.

I frowned at her and whispered in return, "What *what*?"

"What's impossible?"

Gah! I'd spoken aloud again without realizing.

I shook my head. "Sorry. Nothing. Ignore me."

"You're weird." She giggled.

"Shhh."

"Do you talk to yourself often?"

"Be quiet."

"Ladies . . .?"

I stiffened, my blood pressure skyrocketing.

Oh no.

OH NO!

He was looking at us. He'd stopped lecturing and was looking right at us. His hands were on his narrow hips, one of his eyebrows was cocked in displeasure. Also, he was wearing a bowtie.

What the what?

A bowtie?

And yes, he looked hot in a bowtie. How was that even possible?

"Is there something you'd like to share with the rest of the class?"

"Sorry, Professor. We were just debating the finer details of . . ." Taylor glanced at the title of my book, "*Eugene*

Onegin. It won't happen again." Taylor grinned and preened under the singular weight of his attention.

Meanwhile, I sunk lower in my chair, brought my hand to my forehead to obscure my face as much as possible without completely covering it, and shook my head quickly.

The silence that followed was deafening. I didn't dare look up. I was still in the throes of my overreaction and I was sure my cheeks were on fire.

Professor Kroft broke the silence. "Your debate is timely, as *Yevgeniy Onegin* is the first book we'll be discussing."

I closed my eyes; his voice, the words he'd spoken hitting me square in the abdomen, driving the air from my lungs. He'd used the Russian pronunciation of Eugene. Life was not fair. Not only did he look good in leather pants, fabulous in a suit with a bowtie, was a world expert on Russian literature, but also he apparently spoke Russian. Flawlessly.

Flee! He is temptation incarnate! He will steal your soul with sexiness.

"Uh." Taylor's eyes darted around the room and finally, *finally* she shrank back.

"Tell me, Miss . . .?" He paused and I opened one eye, attempting to discern if he was waiting for me or Taylor to provide a last name. Thankfully, his steady gaze was locked on my classmate.

"Taylor Garrison," she supplied, her voice cracking with nerves.

I wanted to shake my head at her in disgust, or shake some sense into her for volunteering a boldfaced lie. Instead, I kept my head down, hoping against hope he'd continue to target bigmouth Taylor.

"And Miss . . .?"

DAMMIT, DOSTOYEVSKY! Why did you have to be so tragic and compelling?

I said nothing, but I might have moaned in mental anguish.

"Miss?" he prompted again, an edge of harassed impatience stealing into the word.

I gathered a large bracing breath—because what else could I do?—and blurted, "Anna Harris."

I waited, but he was silent again. This time the silence stretched much, much longer. It stretched for such a substantial length of time that most of the class turned in their seats to give me the once-over. After they gave me the once-over, they looked between the professor and me, then gave me a twice-over, and a thrice-over.

"Miss Harris," he said finally, like he'd discovered something wonderful for him, and terrible for me.

I opened both my eyes, met the force of his, and grimaced. Yet I managed to choke out, "Professor Kroft."

He smiled—teeth and everything—as he leaned backward onto the table behind him. He tilted his head to the side, crossed his arms, and pinned me with his stare. Rather, he *paralyzed* me with the twin-blue laser beams of sadism pointed at my soul.

Yep.

He recognized me.

And it was obvious he didn't like me very much.

Perhaps he was merely irritated that he'd been interrupted on the first day of class, or perhaps he hadn't liked my hurried departure all those months ago. I couldn't figure out which of my regrettable actions were the culprit.

Either way, whatever the reason, I was in trouble.

"Tell me, Miss Harris, is Pushkin a precursor to the realism later found in the legendary Russian prose novels?"

"Uh," my attention flickered to the side, to Taylor, who was watching me with a please-don't-murder-me expression. She was terrified. For some reason, her terror lessened mine.

"I'm waiting, Miss Harris," he said, demanding my attention once more, in a harsh tone that sent goosebumps racing up my arms and over my chest. "And I don't like to be kept waiting." This last part struck me as meaningful, because I had kept him waiting. I'd kept him waiting last February for twenty minutes before he'd given up and left.

But this wasn't February and this room wasn't a restaurant. I needed to answer, because everyone was waiting. Shaking my head, I blinked rapidly, endeavoring to clear the riot of flailing cobwebs from my mind, and repeated his question silently.

Is Pushkin a precursor to the realism later found in the legendary Russian prose novels?

Yes.

Yes, he is.

I nodded.

He frowned.

I flinched.

Say something. Answer him. You can do this. You love discussing this stuff.

"Um, so, realism. Yes." I nodded again, my mind finally engaging. "Yes, Pushkin is a precursor to the realism found later in prose novels."

"Why?" he asked.

"Why?" I parroted, my voice cracking.

His gaze grew hooded, his jaw slid to the side, his teeth scraping together. "Yes. Why?" The question was now a harsh staccato. Exacting. Punishing.

I answered without allowing myself to overthink, sensing that haste in responding was the only thing keeping me from being tossed out in abject humiliation. "Because he described the differences in social classes during his time. And not just easily discernible differences. He described their lives, everything from high society, to lower gentry, to peasants in the countryside. He displayed a proto-realist attitude later adopted by other authors."

The last syllable of my last word seemed to echo in the room. Or maybe it echoed in my head. Once again, silence stretched.

Professor Kroft's features had arranged themselves into a stoic mask as he continued to stare at me through half-lidded eyes. I was holding my breath. It might have been my imagination, but I was pretty sure half the class was as well.

Finally, he announced, "That is correct."

His gaze shifted from mine, releasing me from the purgatory of his austere attention. "We may find examples of this attention to detail in his tour through Petersburg high-society life with Yevgeniy in the first chapter, and the bucolic descriptions of the provincial nobility," he continued.

I took the opportunity to breathe.

My heart was still racing, but heady relief pumped through my veins. He could still toss me out. He could eject me from the class. He could ridicule and embarrass me.

But I didn't think he would. At least, not today. My heart began a slow descent to the floor as I watched him pace in front of the class, waxing poetic about *quotidian elements*.

I had to drop the course.

I'd read the reality in his eyes when he'd challenged me. They'd glowed with a keen, sinister attentiveness. If I stayed, if I tried to finish the semester, he would make my life extremely unpleasant.

Embrace the wretchedness, Anna. Embrace it.

I'd just resigned myself to embracing wretchedness when I felt eyes on me again. I looked up from the sad faces I'd been doodling in my notebook and discovered I was, once again, the focus of the entire class and Professor Kroft.

"Miss Harris?" His tone was studiously polite. The politeness struck me as infinitely more dangerous than his palpable exasperation earlier.

"Yes?" I croaked, gripping the desk again, hoping he wasn't about to toss me out of the lecture hall.

He held my gaze, and I swear one side of his mouth inched slightly upward with a knowing smirk, though his expression hadn't altered.

"Please stay after class, Miss Harris."

A low murmur rumbled through the hall at the professor's demand framed as a request. Instinctively, I sunk lower in my seat, shying away from the multitude of eyes pointed at me, and gritted my teeth.

Great. Just . . . *great*.

Not even embracing the wretchedness could cheer me up.

Dammit, Dostoyevsky. Damn you to heck.

PART 4

** ANNA **

*I*n Ivan Turgenev's *Fathers and Sons,* there's a scene where Bazarov realized his strict nihilist philosophies and assumptions about the values of provincial life might be erroneous. His entire worldview was challenged, and he was forced to accept that his radical ideas and how he had wielded the sword of his charisma may have irrevocably hurt those who trusted him.

And then—spoiler alert—he contracts blood poisoning and dies.

It's a terrible moment.

However, I was sure that this moment, right now in *my* life, rivaled his moment. At least to me it did.

As my fellow classmates departed, I felt my will to live go with them.

Sorry. That was melodramatic. Let me clarify: I didn't want to die, I wanted to be unconscious. I wished for a blood illness, albeit a temporary one. I'd even settle for a good old-fashioned fainting spell.

If only I had an autopsy to perform—like Bazarov, in

Fathers and Sons—it certainly would have been an excellent excuse to flee.

Sorry. Can't stay. I have a cadaver in my car.

Instead, after I finished packing my bag, I sat still as a statue. I folded my hands on my lap and waited, staring at the top of my desk. My mortification plus the anticipation of what was to come fashioned a figurative blood illness within me, overheating my skin and making me shiver.

Professor Kroft was motionless as well, except he wasn't sitting. He was leaning against the long table at the front of the room, his arms crossed over his broad chest. He'd removed his jacket during the two-hour lecture, which left him in a charcoal-gray vest, white dress shirt, and gray bowtie. He'd also rolled up his shirtsleeves, presumably so he could write on the dry-erase board with ease.

The last of my classmates' footsteps echoed through the nearly empty lecture hall, trailing away until the door closed with a resounding click. My brain reminded me that the doors were locked.

No one could get in.

We were utterly alone and wouldn't be interrupted.

Neither of us made a sound, not at first, although I'm sure my bracing facial expression and averted gaze spoke volumes.

I wanted to leave. The urge to flee was strong. Like the dark side of the Force, it called to me, promised me cookies. The only thing keeping me in my seat was the fact that he was a professor. A tenured professor. My instincts and upbringing demanded I stay and accept the reprimand.

"Come here." His voice echoed in the hall and I started at the command, my eyes lifting from the top of my desk to clash with his.

His gaze was . . . I don't even know how to describe it.

36

Not exactly probing, but not precisely attentive either. He scrutinized me and yet looked bored.

God, let this be over quickly. You cancelled both Still Star-Crossed *and* Arrested Development. *Haven't I suffered enough?*

Recognizing that the time was now, I stood and slung my backpack over my shoulder. I then traversed the stairs leading to the front of the hall, where Professor Leather Pants waited, halting just after the bottom step. With the weight of his gaze following each of my movements, I'm shocked I didn't tumble down the steps, ass over ankles.

My heart thrummed between my ears and in my throat. One thing was for certain: I would not be the first to speak. Mostly because I didn't know what to say. Therefore, rather than exacerbate the situation with inarticulate apologies, I decided silence was the best course of action.

He unfolded his arms and scratched the back of his neck, his stare narrowing until the glacial blue of his irises were small slits. My attention snagged on his forearm. I suspected the baring of his forearms earlier had been an attempt at torture. His forearms were magnificent. And so were his hands. Not that I was staring at them.

Nope. Not staring. Just looking. *Yep.*

"Anna," he said, making me blink his face back into focus.

"Yes?" I squeaked. Again, I was startled. This time by the use of my first name.

He studied me for a protracted moment before stating, "You've read Onegin."

I nodded and said, "Yes," even though he hadn't asked me a question.

"Which of the others on the class syllabus have you already read?"

I shifted my weight from one foot to the other, confused. He didn't sound angry. That was good, right?

"Uh, let's see," I fiddled with the strap of my bag, "Maybe it would be better for me to list which of the books on the syllabus I haven't read."

One side of his mouth hitched upward. "Fine."

"Okay, so, um. I haven't read Nikolai Chernyshevsky's *What Is to Be Done?* Or Maxim Gorky's *Mother*." I tried not to butcher the name Chernyshevsky, but it was ultimately impossible. I had no idea which syllable deserved the emphasis.

He waited for me to continue with my list, his eyebrows lifting by millimeters when I remained silent.

"That's it?"

I nodded.

"Those are the only two you haven't read?"

I nodded again.

He seemed to be gritting his teeth while his gaze flickered down and then up my body. "Did you know it was me?"

My lips parted while my eyebrows danced on my forehead; I didn't understand his question. "Pardon?"

Professor Kroft pushed away from the table, stuffing his fine fingers into his pants pockets, and strolled forward, his gaze searching.

"In February. Did you know who I was?"

I tried to take a step back only for my heel to connect with the stair behind me. "Uh, no. No, I had no idea. I thought you were just a biker dude, or something." My thwarted retreat might have been responsible for the unrehearsed, blunt honesty of my words.

He slowed his advance, both sides of his mouth curving upward for a split second before he erased the almost smile from his face.

"But you figured it out eventually?"

I shook my head again, bracing my feet apart to stand my ground. "No. I had no idea you were a professor. Not until today."

"Then why are you in this class?" he demanded quietly, three feet separating us; the size of his frame made his proximity feel imposing.

"Because I like tragic stories." More unrehearsed and clumsy honesty.

"Tragic stories?"

"Yes."

He frowned, like he was thinking, or trying to remember. "In your email you said you were a romantic."

"I am."

"But you like tragic stories."

I nodded.

He scowled. "That makes no sense."

"It does. The most romantic stories always have tragic elements."

"Like what?"

"*War and Peace.*"

It might have been my imagination, but I could've sworn he swayed toward me. But then he said, "That's ludicrous. *War and Peace* isn't romantic."

I didn't like his tone—it was dismissive—like he thought I was an idiot.

I stiffened my spine and lifted my chin. "It is."

He shifted a step closer, shaking his head, taunting me. "It's Tolstoy's naturalist reflection on inequality and the inevitable disappointment of life. It's about the stark pragmatism required to navigate a reality ripe with injustice. It's about settling. *War and Peace* is brilliant because of the very fact that it's an anti-romance."

What?

Oh, HELL no.

Those were fighting words.

"Then why does it make me feel so much?" I blurted fervently, clutching my chest, clearly forgetting to whom I was speaking. "Why then does Pierre's love for Natasha—"

"Natasha is a faithless twit and Pierre is vapid and brainless. She didn't belong with Pierre, she belonged with Andrei, but she was blind and selfish and she ruined him."

My mouth fell open, wide with outrage. *Sacrilege!*

"I can't believe you just said that."

He shrugged, unconcerned, but his eyes seemed to brighten as they examined me. He smirked, looking more like *some biker dude* in that moment than like a PhD professor in Russian Literature.

"Like Andrei, everybody who is worthwhile or interesting dies before their time. That's how real life works."

"I would argue that the canvas of death and tragedy provides depth to the growth of the characters and underlying romanticism."

"Then you're delusional. And a masochist."

"Then you're a sociopath," I volleyed back, shoving my face in his because he was pissing me off, "incapable of feeling empathy or passion."

His eyes narrowed menacingly as they flared, flickering to my mouth and chasing my anger with something equally hot and confusing.

"You think so?" he rasped on a whisper; it sounded like a challenge. Or a dare. Or both.

"It's a definite possibility." My words arrived breathless because my heart was beating erratically.

His body swayed toward mine again and this time it wasn't my imagination.

What is happening? What is going on?

We shared a breath. And then two breaths. Our eyes clashed. His darkened. The muscle at his jaw ticked. My stomach did a somersault and the back of my throat burned with anticipation.

I felt a tug, a pull, a force, again gravity—like before when we first met—urging me to touch him, to place a hand on his magnificent forearm, to incline my chin just two inches.

Do it!

I can't.

Why not?

He's my professor.

And?

And he's still not my kind of nice.

How do you know?

Just look at his forearms!

. . . sigh.

I was the first to blink.

I lowered my face and turned, breaking the tense moment. My curls fell forward, obscuring me, and I leaned away. Confusion, and something akin to fear, tasted bitter in my mouth. Uncertain what to do next, I improvised.

"Anyway," I endeavored to say, but it sounded garbled and shaky, my heart beating as though I'd run ten miles. I cleared my throat and tried again, "Anyway, I, um," I tossed my thumb over my shoulder, "I'm leaving."

Still confused, still caught in his gravitational field, I loitered for a moment, my eyes on the floor. He was torturously close. Some perverse impulse had me glancing up just as I turned for the stairs. His eyes were still trained on me—now hooded, but no less intense.

My thundering heart twisted and jumped to my throat. I tore my gaze away.

Jeez. This guy.

I'd made it halfway to the door when he called after me, "Are you going to drop the class?"

I halted, tugging my bag higher on my shoulder, and gave him my profile. I couldn't look at him, not yet. I blamed the bowtie. It should have decreased his attractiveness, but instead it was the equivalent of his wearing leather pants.

No one looks good in leather pants.

No one looks good in a bowtie.

But he did.

Frazzled, I admitted, "I don't want to drop the class. I like . . . the subject."

"Fine." His tone was clipped, succinct, like everything was settled. "I'll see you on Wednesday."

I rolled my lips between my teeth, still undecided, and eventually asked the most relevant question bouncing around my brain, "Are you going to pick on me? If I stay?"

It took him a beat to respond. When he did, his tone sounded steady and flat. "Not any more or less than my other students."

I nodded, but confusion distracted me. I was sluggish. What precisely had just happened between us? Had we been about to kiss? Had he wanted to kiss me? Had I imagined that? Had I wanted to kiss him?

I meant, yes. I wanted to kiss him, *theoretically*. But in reality, the kissing of Professor Kroft would be anchored in complications and drama.

He's your professor. You don't kiss your professor. It isn't a thing. In fact, it's an anti-thing.

"Anna."

I shook myself, realizing I'd been lost untangling my bewilderment instead of moving.

I sprinted up the stairs, calling over my shoulder, "Yes. Sorry. I'm leaving. See you later," and bolted out the door, running to my car.

I didn't stop running until my rusted Civic came into view. And then I stopped, berating myself for running, because now I had one of those god-awful stitches in my side. I was not a runner. I could power walk like a boss, but I never ran. Never.

However, considering the fact that I'd just run away from Luca Kroft—for a *second* time—clearly I made an exception for misanthropic men, who looked outstanding in leather pants and bowties.

PART 5

"*L*uca."

I gave my sister my eyes. "Hmm?"

"You're distracted." She hovered by the inglenook, her stare teasing.

"Pardon me. What were you saying?"

"What's the last thing you heard?" Dominika set her hands on her hips.

Pressing my index and middle finger to the space between my eyebrows, I struggled to locate my concentration; it had gone missing on Monday—the first day of summer session—and had further deteriorated on Wednesday, when Anna I. Harris had neglected to show up for my lecture.

Forcing myself into the present, I searched my memory. "You were discussing budgets."

My sister examined me, her eyes growing brighter. "I should know better than to speak of numbers. They're like an off switch for your brain."

I dropped my hand to my lap. "I apologize. Please, thrill me with your impressive numbers."

"It's too late, you lost your chance. Now you'll never

know what I plan to spend on staples for the family's new offices downtown, or how much it costs to purchase ten desk chairs."

I curled my fingers into a fist. "Damn."

She laughed, shaking her head. "You'll come crying to me when you get that huge State Department grant and need help sorting the budget."

Dismissing her statement, I shook my head again to clear it. "Tell me about your budget, I promise to listen."

"No. It's too late, I've moved on from that. The last thing I said was that you better shave, the reservation is at six." Dominika gestured vaguely to my jaw. "But never mind about that, we can be late. Tell me why you're distracted."

A memory manifested as hesitation. Unable to redirect my thoughts, I recalled the colors of her eyes. Again.

A ring of dark russet, a ring of malachite and jade, a starburst of gold and sienna.

We'd been standing close, too close, and her words—the palpable enthusiasm and erudition—had been equally distracting. Our conversation from Monday, truncated though it was, repeated ceaselessly in my mind, a reprise that hadn't yet grown weary or tiresome. Instead, the memory now seemed familiar.

A favorite melody.

An unruly disruption.

But then, Anna had been absent on Wednesday.

Strolling to me, Dominika's stare widened. "Is there something wrong? With your book? Or work? Or has Dad been making life difficult?"

"No." I considered the matter of our father, capitulating to the urge to frown and amending my answer, "Not more than usual."

"Has he been meddling?"

"He always meddles." My relationship with Sergey Kroft was a complicated one, and one which I would never wish on another person.

"I know you enjoy your status as a brooding enigma, but talking to someone you trust—i.e. your impressive older sister—can be helpful."

I met her gaze, saying nothing. Calling me an enigma was more teasing. She'd always accused me of being a terrible liar and unable to veil my thoughts, especially when I most wished to keep them concealed.

"Fine. Twenty questions it is. Is it a person, place, or thing?"

"Dominika."

"Did you find a weird shaped mole? Do you need me to look at it?"

I exhaled a laugh.

"Do you have questions about bees? Or birds? Or—"

"I—"

"—sexual intercourse?"

She wasn't going to stop, which led me to abruptly confess, "Fine. I met someone."

"Oh?" My sister tried to keep her tone light, but I could guess her thoughts. She'd never liked the women I chose. "Do tell," she requested on a sigh, without enthusiasm.

"There's nothing to tell."

Inspecting me, she dropped to the couch, as though gravity had suddenly rendered her unable to stand. "I assume she's like the rest."

"The rest."

Dominika waved her hand in the air, then let it fall to the back of the sofa. "Your type."

"I don't have a type."

"Come off it, Luca." She shoved my shoulder. "You know you do."

"Enlighten me."

"You know, overly educated and . . . delicate." Dominika studied her nails. "Dad loves your broken birds. It's the only thing you and he have in common."

I ignored her comment about our father's taste in women. "Delicate?"

"Yeah, like Sonja. Fragile. Cries a lot. Quivering lips and wobbly chins."

Instinct demanded that I argue with my sister's assessment, but I couldn't. Sonja had been fragile. And needy. And insecure. And had cried a lot. But she'd also been brilliant.

"You like to rescue, Luca. You always have. You never chase. You watch and wait until the weakest is separated from the pack, then you swoop in." Again, she used her hand for emphasis, pushing her stiff fingers through the air as though to mimic a bird or an airplane. My sister glanced to me and promptly tilted her head to the side, rolling her eyes. "Why are you looking at me like that?"

"You've just accused me of having a type, and that type is the weakest link. If my expression distresses you, I have no plans to apologize."

"They're not *weak*, they're. . ." She directed her eyes to the ceiling, not finishing her thought.

"Fragile?"

"Yes."

My glare intensified. "Fragile is a synonym for weak."

Her grin was impertinent. "It's also a synonym for delicate."

"Dominika—"

"And refined!" She sat forward. "Delicate and refined, that's your type. Women with good manners and excellent taste in throw pillows, who never raise their voices, and cry into handkerchiefs. So tell me about this new woman who has you so preoccupied. Talking about her frail nerves will help."

Continuing to glare at my sister, I considered it, mostly because she was so entirely wrong about Anna. And perhaps discussing it would disperse the tension and break the repetition of my thoughts.

She shoved my shoulder again, "Don't take this the wrong way, but—"

"'I scarce ever heard or saw the introductory words, "Without vanity, I may say," etc., but some vain thing immediately followed.'"

Dominika's eyelids lowered slowly. "Why are you quoting Benjamin Franklin to me?"

"If you're moved to preface your thoughts with a disclaimer, the words that follow will always be of the exact nature you seek to avoid. So if you tell me, 'Don't take this the wrong way,' invariably, it is something that I will *take the wrong way*."

She gave me a grunt of irritation. "You are a grouch."

"And you don't want me to take that the wrong way?"

"No. Take that the wrong way—you are a grouch—I meant it the wrong way. But what I *was* going to say—which you should *not* take the wrong way—is that, before you get too serious about this one, maybe ask yourself the question: why do I seek out women who are the human equivalent of a wet blanket?"

"Because I'm a grouch?"

She blinked at me twice, very, very slowly. "Never mind. You're right. You deserve to sleep next to a wet, chilly blanket. You have my blessing to pursue whatever limp, delicate flower has caught your interest now."

Dominika's theatrics caused me to speak without thinking, wanting to defend Anna without understanding the urge. "Anna isn't like that."

"Which part? The limp part or the delicate flower part?"

"Neither."

"Oh yeah? What's she like?"

I opened my mouth to respond, to tell my sister that Anna was full of vibrancy, that she'd surprised me with her honesty, soul, and intellect. And passion.

When we'd met in February, my stare had lingered against my will. As though compelled, I'd memorized the shape of her lips, the graceful line of her jaw and neck, the warm mahogany of her curly hair. She'd captivated me.

And then she left after I confessed the truth.

"To use your analogy," I hedged, picking my words carefully, "she's not a wet blanket, at all."

"Really?" My sister sounded unconvinced. "What is she then? A damp blanket? Moist, maybe?"

"An electric blanket."

Dominika frowned suddenly, her eyes now sharp and interested, and she leaned forward slowly. "You mean she smells faintly of burnt hair?"

"No." I focused on the arm of my couch, on a red mark I'd inadvertently made while grading papers last year. "She smells like wildflowers and quiet libraries, redolent of peace and exuberance."

I looked to my sister and found her expression sober.

"Dad wouldn't like that."

"No. I don't imagine he and Anna would get along at all." I smirked at the thought. She was far too independent, of both mind and spirit. He'd never countenance her individuality.

"Tell me more."

"It matters not at all." Looking back to the red mark, I clenched my teeth. "She's my student."

In my peripheral vision, I saw Dominika's jaw drop. She pushed herself to the edge of the sofa. "Oh my God, are you serious?"

I nodded, glaring over my sister's head to the shelves of books lining the wall. "She's in my summer session."

"Luca." Dominika's mouth remained agape, clearly struggling to speak. "How much younger is she?"

"Ten years." I'd researched Anna after our abbreviated meeting in February, after experiencing a great deal of difficulty putting her from my mind. It was her email, I'd decided, that made dismissing her abandonment of me impossible.

Thus, I decided to wait before contacting her again. According to her transcript—which was impeccable—she had another eighteen months as a student. If my thoughts continued to drift toward her after she graduated, the plan was to reach out to her then.

"That's not too bad. But you can't date a student. You can't. You know how you are."

"I know."

"I mean, professors can date students. It's discouraged, but allowed. But, don't. Don't do it." My sister grabbed my arm, forcing me to meet her eyes. "You fall so hard. My lovely, lonely boy. You're all heart and soul. You crush yourself."

She didn't need to tell me this; I was fully aware of my faults and history. Yet her words merely served to demonstrate how woefully she misunderstood my nature.

Perhaps others, cut from different cloth, could pick and choose their conquests. Live their lives as patient fishermen, searching with intermittent success within a vast sea full of alluring fish. If the circumstances of one catch proved inconvenient, these fictional fishermen need only toss back the lure and wait for another.

Not so for me.

I vehemently rejected this belief that our souls could thrive with any number of partners, a good-enough *rodstvennaya dusha*.

One.

One half of one soul.

It is popular to say that one must find love within oneself before knowing how to love another. I rejected this statement outright, as both imbecilic in theory and impossible in practice.

Thus, I'd searched where I thought my *rodstvennaya dusha* would most likely be, becoming entangled several times, but never so much that the thorns of the hedgerow ensnared me beyond reason, beyond ability to rejoin my previous path.

I hadn't found her, or anything close. And that—the disappointment, the continued vacancy, *not* the thorny hedgerow— had left me crushed.

However, I understood Dominika's worry. In her eyes I would always be the younger brother she'd had to raise and protect, crying for his mother.

"I assume she's a literature major? Think of what it would be like for her, the power imbalance. She'd be looking at you with stars in her eyes, hero worship, and not your normal hero worship from these wet fragile blankets you've chosen in the past—you know what I mean. Think about it from her perspective. That kind of dynamic wouldn't be good for either of you. And it wouldn't last. You need to protect yourself, and her."

"I know."

I didn't correct her assumption that Anna's major was literature; in the scheme of this conversation, that detail was minor in comparison to the behemoth difference in our—as Dominika labeled it—power dynamic.

I was her professor, her *teacher*. I took this charge seriously, a sacred trust, never to be tarnished by selfish interest. This alone placed her well beyond my reach.

And yet . . .

Interest remained. Steadfast, undeniably selfish, and—recently, since Monday—unmanageable. Burdensome in a way that felt like a punishment.

"What are you going to do?" Her fingers flexed on my arm.

I covered her hand with mine, knowing I should reassure her, but resigned to my inability to lie.

Thus, I settled for the truth. "Nothing, Dominika. I'm going to do nothing."

PART 6

** ANNA **

I didn't go to class on Wednesday.

Instead, I went to the movies. Alone.

Now it was Friday and I had until 11:59 p.m. to decide whether or not to drop the class. I didn't know what to do.

And I was rushing. I was rushing everywhere. I'd rushed through my shower this morning, brushing my teeth, getting dressed. My socks didn't match and, based on the way my underwear tugged unnaturally, I was pretty sure I'd put it on backwards.

At present, I'd just rushed into work. I wasn't late. I was ten minutes early.

"Hey, Anna. How was your week?"

Oh, you know, reading, rollerblading, puzzles; on Monday I almost kissed my hot professor, and on Tuesday I went to trivia night and won second place in the semi-finals. The usual.

"Fine. Good. Fine," I said too loudly and in a voice much higher than my normal tone.

My boss, Tim, gave me a perplexed smile. "Are you okay?"

I nodded, tying on my apron. "I'm good. Fine. Good. Fine."

He stared at me for another few seconds, then shrugged. "Okay, so, you're in zone four tonight and we have two big-top reservations. One for twelve, the other for twenty. Sasha will be with you and Frank will bus."

I nodded as Tim spoke, and kept on nodding after he was finished, forcing myself to absorb his words.

Zone four, two big parties, one table for twelve, one table for twenty, Sasha would be helping me, and Frank would be bussing the tables.

"Got it. Sounds good." I gave Tim two thumbs up.

He glanced at my thumbs and then at me. "Are you sure you're okay? You seem anxious."

I tried to swallow, but I rushed it, and experienced a swallow misfire. It took every ounce of my self-control not to cough.

Instead, I rasped, "Sure, yeah, good. I'm good."

Tim wrinkled his nose, his eyebrows forming a deep V on his forehead. "Well, maybe cut back on the coffee then."

As a server, if you rush, you make mistakes. A fact I'd learned the hard way. This job had taught me how to pause and reflect before taking action, because the alternative was spilling seven beers on yourself while jogging across the dining room.

"Sure thing, boss." I stuffed my hands in my pockets and nodded once slowly. My slow nod seemed to pacify him because he walked away with less concern plaguing his features.

As soon as he was out of sight, I coughed and cleared my throat until I could swallow again.

He was right.

I was anxious.

I was anxiously obsessing about what to do.

I hadn't told anyone about my *encounter* with Professor Kroft. Not even Emily. I didn't want to get him in trouble. Or . . . something.

He didn't do anything wrong.

He hadn't. We hadn't kissed. He hadn't touched me or said anything inappropriate.

But still. Still.

STILL!

Of note, I *accidentally* looked up the university's policy on fraternization. There I was, minding my own business, when *BAM!* the Internet navigated to the university's guidance on the subject of relationships between professors and students.

Since the web page was already up, I decided to read it. What could be the harm in that?

The university's policy was ambiguous. As consenting adults, fraternization was not forbidden. But faculty (and staff) were encouraged to avoid "practices and behaviors that give the appearance of favoritism, harassment, or discrimination." Of course, true favoritism, harassment, and discrimination were outright prohibited, not to mention usually illegal.

Either way, it didn't matter.

If I dropped the class, I would never see him again. Problem solved.

If I didn't drop the class, then he would be my pessimistic professor, and I would be his quixotic student for the next ten weeks, and that would be that. Problem also solved . . . *sorta.*

I pushed my obsessive thoughts to the deep recesses of my mind—where I stored information about folding sheets correctly and how to be a proper lady—and occupied myself with work, being mindful not to rush.

Immersing myself in waiting tables did the trick. I'd

completely forgotten about the class and Professor Leather Pants until I saw him.

. . . *wait! WHAT?*

I strolled out of the kitchen alcove, ready to welcome the table of twenty that had just been seated, when I spotted him. I had no other choice but to jump behind a potted plastic tree and do a double take, hoping against hope that the super hottie in black pants and a black dress shirt was not my professor.

Apparently, hope is for hipsters because hope failed me.

He was sitting in the chair closest to the kitchen and facing the alcove, I had a clear view. His hair was elegantly styled rather than spiked like it had been at Jake Peterson's Microbrewery, or natural and loose like it had been in class. He was also without bowtie or leather pants, as far as I could tell. But it was definitely Professor Kroft.

And he was sitting among nineteen other people at one long table. In my section.

Why me? WHY ME??

Oh the wretchedness.

"What's going on? What are you waiting for? Do you want me to get their drinks?" Sasha stopped next to me, already frantic.

Five years older than me and an underserver, Sasha hadn't quite learned how to be mindful. She was panicky and we hadn't even taken their orders yet.

"Calm down, Sasha-frantic." I patted her shoulder, still peering at the table where the professor sat. Next to him was a very, very pretty woman who looked a lot like him: same blonde hair, same blue eyes, same mouth. Different nose, though.

Unless they were one of those creepy brother-sister couples—you know, the ones that aren't related but look like they could be—this woman was his actual sister. Which meant he was out with his family.

"Anna? What are you doing?"

I straightened my shoulders and tried to shake off my creeper complex. "This is what we're going to do: I'm going to take the drink orders. You go grab some bread, butter, and water for the table. When you come out, I'll give you the orders I've taken so far, you enter them and wait at the bar for the order. I'll enter the rest so—hopefully—everything will be ready at the same time. I'll carry out the first load, you get the second. Meanwhile, I'll tell them about the specials, and so forth. Sound good?"

She nodded. "I can do this."

I grabbed her shoulders and gave her a reassuring squeeze. "You can, Sasha. You can do this. You are Sasha-fantastic."

I turned from my coworker, lifted my chin, and prepared to meet my doom.

Or wretchedness.

Or just the really, really uncomfortable next few minutes.

As I approached, I eyeballed the rest of the table. They were all dressed really nicely, like designer-cut suits on the guys and more diamonds than I'd seen outside the Tower of London on the women. Luca's sister—or cousin or whatever—wore a diamond necklace and matching earrings. The older woman across from him had on three diamond bracelets and a stone on her third finger the size of a marble.

Holy WOW.

I forced myself to look away. That rock would hurt in a fistfight.

I didn't know if he was looking at me or not. I didn't check. Instead, I walked to the opposite side of the long table.

"Hello. May I start you off with something to drink?"

A woman in her mid-thirties glanced at me and offered a sincere smile. "Please. You have Zyr Vodka, yes?"

"Yes. Yes, we do." I endeavored to hide my surprise. She had a Russian accent.

"Zyr martini on the rocks, please."

I nodded and moved to the man on her right, repeated the same question and was met with a similar response. With each person I worked myself closer to Luca, but I dared not look at him. Five Zyr Vodka martinis, two white wines, and one bottle of champagne later, I gathered a deep breath and lifted my eyes to him.

He wasn't looking at me.

I blinked at his profile and then forced myself to say, "May I start you off with something to drink, sir?"

"Vodka, neat. Tito's if you have it, Zyr if you don't." He waved a dismissive hand in my direction, then continued his discussion with the older woman across from him. You know, the one you'd want on your side in a fistfight because of the rock on her finger.

But back to Professor Passionless.

I didn't know what to expect, but I hadn't expected detachment. Again, I stared at his profile.

Thank God Sasha chose that precise moment to tap on my shoulder so I could pass her the first of the drink orders. Otherwise, I might have spent the rest of the night standing there, glowering at him.

Shaking my head to clear it, I moved to the other side of the table and continued. I felt eyes on me, but mindfully told myself I was imagining things. Nevertheless, by the time I finished collecting all the orders, my cheeks were burning, and I had the sensation of non-gross creepy-crawly things on the back of my neck, like a finger whispering down my spine.

"Did you get the rest of the drink orders?" Sasha asked as I walked to where she was waiting at the bar.

"I did."

"Was it my imagination, or did, like, half of those people have Russian accents?"

I shrugged, evading her question. She was wrong, sixteen of them had an accent, well over half. But about half of them were speaking in Russian.

I was in a tangle of feelings by the time I made it back to the table with the first of their drinks and being mindful was becoming increasingly difficult. But I would persevere and relay the specials, even if it killed me.

Which, unless that woman with the ring punched me in the temple for running out of halibut, relaying the specials probably wouldn't kill me.

"Good evening," I addressed the half of the table where Luca wasn't, plastering a mild smile on my features before recapping the specials. I wrote down the first ten orders, growing calmer as I answered questions about the menu.

Then I was off to the other side. I kept my gaze focused on the deathbringer—what I'd nicknamed the large diamond ring on the older woman's hand—while I launched into the same spiel I'd given to the first half of the table, finishing with, "Can I interest you in our seasonal steamed clams to start? Or the escargot?"

"How are the snails cooked?" Luca asked, making me jump a little.

I swallowed a tremor of nerves and lifted my eyes to his. Unsurprisingly, he was looking at me. Other than the looking, I had no expectations. Therefore, the glint of challenge in his eyes and the barely there hovering smile were neither surprising nor unsurprising.

They were flustering.

I cleared my throat before responding, "The escargot are served Bourguignon style, with butter and garlic."

"What about the halibut? I saw it was one of the specials, but you didn't list it."

My smile grew brittle. "We're out of the halibut. We have bass instead."

"How is the bass prepared again?"

I opened my mouth to respond, but the one wielding the deathbringer cut me off. "Luca, you don't even like bass. Leave the pretty girl alone and stop quizzing her. She's not one of your students to torture."

His eyes cut to mine again, pinning me, sending a jolt of scorching *hello* and *you're in trouble* and maybe also *hot for teacher* to the pit of my stomach.

Meanwhile, the woman sitting next to him spoke up, "Ignore him. My brother is just enamored with you and lacks basic people skills."

"Dominika," he growled.

She disregarded his warning. "I apologize for his bad behavior. Here, he'll have the salmon with risotto cake, *I'll* have the bass, and you can ignore him for the rest of the evening."

I glanced at her wide, apologetic smile as she handed me her menu. I accepted it with a garbled thanks, new feelings surfacing to tangle my throat and thoughts. Somehow I managed to jot down the rest of the orders without asking his sister to repeat the part where she'd said, *he's enamored with you* so I could record it.

Like the professional I was, I turned from the table graciously, crossed the dining room with an even stride, and then hid behind the potted plant so I could ogle him from behind a fake tree.

He looked unhappy. He was leaning back in his chair as

though relaxed, but the frown marring his features gave him away. His sister was laughing and nudging him with her elbow. Not to be outdone, deathbringer glinted in the candle light.

"Anna? Did they order? I was about to go refill water glasses."

"Go ahead. I'll enter the order." I waved Sasha off, unwilling to remove my eyes from Luca's stern expression.

Leather pants. Bowties. Stern expressions. All things that shouldn't be attractive, but were damn sexy on Luca Kroft.

PART 7

** ANNA **

"Someone tell me about the relationship between the story and the way it's told in Pushkin's *The Queen of Spades*."

I lifted my hand in the air.

"Anyone?" Luca's gaze swept over the class, sliding over my extended hand as though it were invisible.

Gritting my teeth, I waved my fingers. Just a tad. I even tried to lengthen my arm by sitting forward in my seat.

"Not even a guess?" He regarded the lecture hall with disappointment. When no one else moved, he pulled out the class roster. "Emma Nixon. Tell me about *The Queen of Spades* and why Pushkin's method of telling the story is as important as the story itself."

His target sat directly in front of me. I watched as she straightened and fiddled with the pencil she held.

"Is this about his use of numbers? Because I didn't understand that." Emma was a good student, just not great with the philosophical models characteristic of Russian literature.

I let my hand fall quietly to the tabletop and tried to hide my frown. I didn't know why I bothered anymore. Four weeks into the semester and he hadn't called on me since that first day.

Luca tilted his head to one side, considering her. "Do you understand the concepts of fabula and syuzhet?"

Emma shook her head, now twirling the pencil between her fingers with nervous abandon. I could tell she was frustrated by her lack of ability to engage with him. But he took her nerves in stride, re-explaining the concepts in a new way and encouraged her to help him fill in the blanks. He even gave her a small smile of praise when she arrived at the right answer without him having to spell it out.

Bitterness blossomed on my tongue as I watched their exchange. I glanced at the big clock over the board, five minutes left before the end of class. Five tortuous minutes.

Obviously, I hadn't dropped the class three weeks ago when I'd had the chance. If I were being honest with myself, the reason I didn't drop out was because I wanted to see him again.

Also now obvious, Professor Kroft wasn't enamored with me. His sister had been delusional, although I was still inclined to like her.

Meanwhile, I'd become completely enamored with him.

I should have listened to that woman with the ring. You don't get a ring like deathbringer without knowing what's what.

Professor Kroft had both kept and broken the promise he'd made to me weeks ago. He didn't pick on me any more than the other students. The problem was, he didn't pick on me at all. He pretended I didn't exist. And this was a special kind of torture because Luca Kroft was a *fantastic* teacher.

Like, the best I've ever had.

He engaged his students rather than talked at them. He forced them to become a part of the narrative, grow invested in Tolstoy and Gogol. He challenged them to confront their ideas about life, nature, morality, and—yes—even the human soul.

Last week he'd made several groups of students act out a scene from *The Brothers Karamazov*, casting women in the roles of the men, asking them to explain their motivations as though they were the characters. I'd wanted desperately to be chosen for the role of Ivan, but I was passed over, given no role except silent spectator.

So, I guess he did pick on me by not picking on me.

Every week—his charisma, intelligence, patience with and passion for his *other* students—had me falling a little more head over heels. And I wasn't the only one.

Taylor, the troublesome talker from the first class, along with at least seventy-five percent of the other students, had basically become his disciples. The books she'd scoffed at on that first day now littered her desk, pages flagged and earmarked. She'd invited me out to dinner last week with a few of our classmates and we'd spent the entire meal debating the superiority of Tolstoy over his contemporaries.

Luca Kroft had made them all Russian literature zealots.

After each class I'd leave feeling both energized and despondent. I wanted to debate with him, with the other students. I wanted to be a part of what felt like a movement and an awakening. Instead, I'd been relegated to the sidelines.

I was frustrated.

Yet enamored.

Even if I'd never met him months ago in his leather pants, I was pretty darn sure I'd still be smitten with him now.

Abruptly, Luca glanced at his watch. "Ah, times up."

A quiet murmur of regret rippled through the class. This was customary at the end of his lectures. If he heard or noticed it, he never made a sign.

"I have your papers from last week at the front, stacked alphabetically. Letters 'A' through 'H' are here, 'I' through 'M' here, and so forth. Pick them up before you depart. If you have any questions about your grade, schedule an appointment through my secretary."

I perked up at this news. He'd warned us before we turned in our first paper that he was exceptionally critical. Most of us could expect Ds and Cs, but that he anticipated we would improve over time.

Determinedly, I spent every free minute on my paper for a week and a half, crafting it, perfecting it. Plus, I loved the subject matter: Onegin's relationship with the young Tatyana Larina and how the role of superfluous man shaped their combined destiny.

Since Luca refused to call on me during class, I poured every ounce of frustrated thoughts and feelings into the paper.

He left through the side door and I turned to my classmate. "Hey, Taylor? Could you watch my stuff? I'll grab our papers."

"Sure, but—"

Not waiting for the rest of her sentence, I jogged down the steps and power-walked to the front table, waiting my turn for the 'A' through 'H' stack. Upon reaching the papers, I grimaced.

He hadn't been lying about being critical. The top paper —and all the others I flipped through—looked like they'd been bled upon. Red pen colored every page—crossed-out sentences, questions in the margin, culminating into at least a paragraph of comments at the end of each paper, in what I presumed was his scrawling handwriting.

I pulled Taylor's from the stack, noticing how red it was, but making a concerted effort to avoid seeing her final grade.

Then I found mine.

My heart stuttered. And then it dropped to my feet. Adrift, I blinked at my paper, dumbly flipping through the pristine pages.

Except for the final grade—which was a B—he hadn't written on it at all.

Not *at all.* Nothing. No thoughts. No questions. No comments.

A potent mixture of confusion and anger swirled in my stomach. Tears pricked behind my eyes. My hurting heart sent a wave of heat up my neck and to my cheeks.

He'd ignored me.

Again.

"Hey, Anna? Are you done?"

I glanced over my shoulder and realized I was holding up the line. Clutching my paper to my chest, I quickly moved out of the way and numbly climbed the stairs to a waiting Taylor.

"Ah! I'm so nervous. I don't think I did very well." She accepted her paper, flipping through his red marks without reading them and searching for her final grade. "Damn. I got a D."

I gritted my teeth, irritated with Taylor. Actually, I was jealous. She had a treasure trove of Luca's comments and insights, and she'd ignored them, instead focusing on the grade. I wanted to throttle her.

"I did, too," Jordan Washington, the boy who sat on her other side chimed in. "And so did Carter, Jayden, and Gretchen, and everyone I've talked to so far."

"What did you get, Anna?" Taylor eyeballed me, her frowning gaze moving to the paper I held clutched to my chest.

I shrugged and stuffed it into my bag, trying to keep my tone even. "I guess everyone got a D," I said without outright lying.

"Don't take it so hard, Harris," Jordan gave me a sympathetic smile. "He did warn us."

I huffed a bitter laugh, shaking my head but saying nothing, and hoisted my bag to my shoulder. My stomach hurt and my eyes felt scratchy.

"See you guys later." I gave my classmates an uneven wave and, for no reason in particular, walked down the stairs. This would take me to the side door of the lecture hall and into the Russian Studies Department instead of outside and to the parking lot.

I left the large classroom, turning toward the faculty offices—for no reason in particular. I stopped at the reception desk, where the department secretary usually sat, and stared at it. Unsurprisingly, no one was there. Class ended at 8:00 p.m., well after the end of normal business hours.

It took that long—the walk from my desk in the lecture hall to the desk of the department secretary—for my brain to catch up with the intentions of my feet. I scanned the top of the desk, looking for the administrator's business card. My aim was to find her number, call her in the morning, and make an appointment with Professor Kroft, as he'd instructed, to ask about my grade.

Because I had no idea why I'd received a B instead of an A, or a C, or a D, or an F. He'd given me *nothing* to go on.

So, yeah, I had questions about my grade. I also had questions about why he was such an arrogant asshole. Given my state of mind, I decided to make the appointment for next week; hopefully time would help me simmer down so I could focus on my grade, and not his assholeishness.

Something out of the corner of my eye snagged my attention. I glanced to the right just as a blur of movement at the end of the hallway disappeared into an office. I stared at the open door, at least thirty feet from where I was standing. It was a corner office at the end of the hall and the door faced out, toward the secretary.

I spotted a window, a desk, a shelf laden with books, stacks of books next to the desk, and white fringe on a red carpet.

Then I spotted a man walking around in the office. My pulse ticked up, because the man was Luca. I recognized the clothes he was wearing from earlier, but more than that I recognized the way he moved.

I faced the hallway. My feet and my brain discussed the situation very, very briefly, a la:

Feet: *He's right there.*

Brain: *Go get him.*

Feet: *Roger that, we're on our way.*

Then my feet moved me toward the open door of the office. My heart beat loudly between my ears, not with nerves this time but with irrational anger, and the misguided determination that accompanies aforementioned irrational anger.

I halted at the doorway to his office and found him standing in front of an open file cabinet, his profile to me. Tangentially, I noticed his office was large, much larger than the ones I'd been in over the course of my college career. But then most of my courses were in science and engineering, where the buildings were newer, more efficiently designed. This building was over one hundred years old.

Glaring at my professor, I knocked on the doorjamb.

He glanced over his shoulder, his pale blue eyes distracted. And then he did a double take. He stiffened, frowning severely as his attention flickered down and then up my body before capturing my gaze.

He looked . . . guarded.

"Are you lost?" To my ears, he sounded gruff and argumentative.

I shook my head while I stepped into his office, shut the door behind me, and dropped my bag on a brown leather sofa at my side.

Luca's eyes followed my movements as he turned to face me, slowly shutting the file cabinet drawer. He stuffed his fine fingers into his pants pockets. But he said nothing.

I yanked the term paper from my bag and held it up between us. He glanced at it, then moved his guarded scowl back to me.

I had so many questions. So many angry, hurt, irritated, frustrated questions. I had a torrent of them.

Instead, I asked, "You gave me a B?"

He swallowed before responding. "I didn't give you a B, Anna. You earned a B."

I felt my frown intensify. "How so?"

His lips parted as though he was actually going to answer, but I cut him off by obnoxiously balling up the term paper and dropping it in his trash can. He watched me do this, his attention lingering on the waste bin for three or four seconds before he blinked and glared at me again.

"How did I *earn* a B? Tell me, because I have no idea. I have *no idea*."

Luca set his jaw, his eyes narrowing, again regarding me in silence.

Luckily, I didn't need him to respond; the momentum of my anger had carried me too far to listen or to engage in a meaningful discussion. I didn't care what he had to say. I needed to be heard.

"Do you know why I have no idea? Because you give me *nothing*. Nothing. I get nothing from you." My voice broke. I had to clear my throat before I could continue. "You won't call on me in class. You won't even look at me. Why am I suddenly invisible to you?"

"You're not invisible to me."

I huffed a bitter laugh in response, shaking my head, because the last three weeks painted a different picture. Plus, I was too preoccupied with the crushing burden of thoughts and emotions I hadn't realized I was feeling.

"You said you wouldn't pick on me any more or less than your other students, but you lied. You're an outstanding teacher, Luca, but you're also a liar. Why won't you teach me? Everyone else gets to debate with you, share ideas, challenge you, be challenged by you. Everyone else gets papers so covered in red ink with your thoughts and ideas that they look like evidence from a crime scene. But mine is white. Mine is blank. Mine is empty. You give *me* nothing."

An irritating tear rolled down my cheek and I swiped at it angrily, furious with myself for crying even a little.

"Everyone else gets to have you," I whispered brokenly. "And I get nothing."

The muscle at his jaw ticked, but otherwise he remained still. Standing like a perfect, impervious statue. Glaring at me.

I needed a minute before I trusted my voice again and looking at his impassive features made my chest hurt, so I dropped my eyes to the carpet and gathered several steadying, mindful breaths.

What am I even doing here?

My anger deflated in the face of my foolishness, leaving me feeling wretched—truly wretched—and miserable.

What do you hope to accomplish, Anna? You're making a fool of yourself. What do you want from him?

"Something. Anything," I whispered to myself.

That's pathetic. Why are you doing this?

I sighed sadly, the ache in my chest intensifying. I had the sudden sensation of being hollowed out, because the voice inside my head was right. I *was* pathetic. I had ridiculous, unrequited feelings for a statue.

I needed to leave.

I turned from him and reached for my bag, tugging it on my shoulder. I couldn't bring myself to look at him again, so I directed a short wave at the room. "Right. Well . . . as always, thanks for the stimulating chat."

My hand closed over the knob and I'd opened the door just three inches before it was slammed shut again. Luca's open palm was pressed against the wooden door, level with my face. He'd pushed it closed and now stood directly behind me.

I didn't have a moment to register shock, because in the very next second I was turned. He pulled the bag from my arm, pushed my back against the door, and kissed me.

PART 8

＊ ANNA ＊

*H*e groaned.
Or was that me?

Not that it mattered, and not that I possessed the higher brain function at present required to debate the matter, but I was pretty sure we were lost in each other to an equivalent degree.

He kissed me. A deep, searching, demanding kiss that tasted like urgency and annihilated restraint. And he placed his hands on me, under my shirt, his fine fingers digging into the skin of my back, pulling me against him even as he roughly pressed my body against the door with his body.

It took me point-five seconds to move beyond my shock, and when I did my response was instinctual, primitive. I melted against him, opening my mouth and searching for his tongue. I sucked on it, so very hungry for the taste of him, and grabbed fistfuls of his shirt, yanking it from his pants.

Holy *wow*, I didn't care how I got here, how we'd arrived at this moment, but I never wanted it to end. I wanted to drown in him, in the hot, claiming slide of his mouth, in this dizzy combination of euphoria and uncertainty.

I touched him—his glorious stomach, sides, and back—
and shivered at the contact. His muscles tensed beneath my
fingertips, his skin hot, and his body so very reactive to my
touch. Luca made a sound like a growl in the back of his
throat, pressing his thigh insistently between my legs, shifting
it up and then down with a purposeful and brazen movement.
My heart slammed against my ribcage as lust pooled low in
my abdomen.

And then someone knocked on the door.

Three quick raps followed by, "Professor Kroft?"

The voice—close behind me, just beyond the door—
crashed over my brain, body, and libido like a bucket of ice
water. It was Taylor.

Abruptly stiff as a board, I sucked in a startled breath. My
eyes flew open, crashing into his. Comprehending where I
was, who I was with, and what we'd just been doing, a spike
of disbelief and frenzied panic coursed through my veins.

Yet, to my utter surprise, Luca didn't appear at all
flustered.

No. Not panicked.

Not even startled.

More like . . . a heady mixture of insatiability and
irritation.

His stare singed me as he calmly mouthed, *Shhh.*

She knocked again. "It's Taylor. I . . . I wanted to talk to
you about my paper. I saw your car in the parking lot and
thought, if you have a free moment now—"

"Make an appointment." Luca's tone was tight and
controlled. He held my gaze captive, the heat of his palms
still burning my skin.

I sensed my classmate hesitate before responding. "I
would, but I'm usually working during your office
hours and—"

"I'm busy with another student," Luca snapped, his voice now unyielding and laced with hostility. "Make an appointment."

I flinched at the word *student,* my eyes falling to his throat as I tried to swallow. Heat flooded my neck and cheeks.

Crap. Crap. Craaaaaaaaaaaap.

"Oh. Sorry, sorry. I guess I'll schedule an appointment or come back later." Her voice faded, followed by dull footsteps leading away from the door. Meanwhile, I held my breath, staring at his bowtie, battling the crushing wave of turmoil holding my throat and lungs hostage.

His hands were still on my body, wrapped around my waist and digging into my back. Luca's muscular leg still pressed shamelessly against the apex of my thighs. I felt his eyes on me, weighted like a sandbag laying on my chest.

"Anna," he said, drawing my focus to him, his voice just above a whisper.

Even so, I jumped at the sound of my name, my fingers falling from his torso as though caught with my hand in the cookie jar, and I automatically responded, "Professor Kroft."

He winced. And then he closed his eyes. And then he exhaled.

I stared at him, the severely beautiful lines of his face, and attempted to find the right words to express the many colors and shapes of my emotions vying for dominance. I was part elation, part trepidation, and part craving a gin and tonic.

But before I could give voice to my thoughts, Luca stepped back, shoving his hands in his pockets and turning, walking several paces away to the center of his office.

He cleared his throat once, then said in a firm voice, "You should leave."

. . .

. . .

. . .

Ugh.

His words landed like a physical blow and the wind was forced from my lungs, leaving me breathless.

And wretched.

Breathless and Wretched, the new fragrance by Calvin Klein.

My gaze moved over the expanse of his back, his broad shoulders encased in a white dress shirt, presently untucked because of me. He felt distant, much farther away than the five steps he'd placed between us.

If I'd been a different kind of nice, I might've sauntered across the room, slid my arms around him, and whispered naughty alternatives in his ear.

But I wasn't that kind of nice. I was the take-people-at-their-word nice. And he wanted me to leave.

A sharp ache filling my chest, I retrieved my backpack, not quite able to lift it to my shoulder, and turned from the sight of him. A million thoughts circled my brain as I gripped the doorknob and twisted it.

Numbly, I stepped out of the room and pulled the door shut behind me. But I didn't leave. I couldn't. I was caught in a labyrinth of turmoil and indecision, unsure if I was upset by what had happened, by the kiss and by Taylor's disruption, or happy, or relieved, or . . . what I was.

A sound of movement from inside Luca's office spurred my feet into action. I jogged quickly away, down the hall, out of the Russian Studies Department, and outside to tepid heat of a mid-summer evening. As I unlocked my car, wading through my mess of feelings about the kiss and subsequent interruption and rejection, I decided three things:

1. I liked being kissed by Luca Kroft. I liked it a lot. A. Lot.
2. I was upset and angry and (as of yet, some undetermined level of) hurt that he'd dismissed me afterward.
3. We would never be a *we*, because *we* were doomed. I was goofy. And he was . . . not goofy. Again, we were two different kinds of nice, and never the twain shall meet.
4. Because of things 1, 2, and 3—and because my drama-free, sedate existence appealed to me more than hot kisses paired with riding the roller coaster of rejection and failure—I was going to late-withdraw from Professor Kroft's class, thereby greatly reducing the chances of ever seeing him again.
5. Adventures were overrated. I was done with adventures.
6. Worst of all, I still genuinely liked Luca Kroft. I admired him. At least, I admired the version of him he shared freely with everyone but me.

Being perpetually ignored and then rejected by a person I admired made me want to cry into a big pillow and listen to The Cure while watching *Old Yeller* and reading the world statistics about the Zika virus.

But I wouldn't.

Instead, I would act. I would *do something* to extract myself from the overwhelming and oppressive feelings inspired by the last several weeks.

Swallowing thickly, I pulled the smartphone from my bag with unsteady fingers, navigated to my student account, and selected the dropdown box labeled *enrollment status*. Without allowing myself to debate the matter, I chose "late-withdraw" and hit the submit button, waiting just long enough for the next screen to load, confirming my selection, before turning off my phone and stuffing it in my bag.

The interior of my car had become tyrannically hot and judgmental. The word *coward* bounced around my brain, as though the upholstery of my aging Honda Civic had whispered the accusation in my ear.

I ignored the creeping doubt in favor of rewarding my pragmatism and swift action with a new jigsaw puzzle. Puzzles wouldn't kiss me one moment, then push me away the next.

No. Unlike moody, gorgeous, brilliant Russian lit professors, puzzles were safe. Puzzles were solvable. Puzzles didn't move my soul and inspire me to wish for things.

Most importantly, puzzles couldn't break my heart.

PART 9

** ANNA **

I felt better, more at peace with my decision to withdraw as days turned into weeks. Admittedly, I missed listening to the debates during class as well engaging in discussions with my classmates outside of class, because I'd enjoyed the subject matter so much. I also missed Luca. I missed his brilliance. I missed listening to his lectures. I missed being challenged on a visceral level.

But gone were the emotional highs and lows associated with seeing him and being ignored by him. Gone were the weekly disappointments as well as the thrill of being inspired.

Ah well.

Such was the life of an unrepentant tranquility-monger.

Therefore, peace reigned and all was as it should be . . . until I received a call from my advisor.

"There's no easy way to say this, Anna, so I'm just going to give it to you straight. Professor Kroft is challenging your late-withdraw."

I frowned at the half-solved ten-thousand-piece puzzle littering my kitchen table, the one I'd purchased to congratulate myself on my quick and pragmatic thinking.

"What does that mean?"

"It means he says you didn't discuss the withdrawal with him ahead of time and he isn't allowing it."

"Isn't allowing it? Why does he have a say?"

"Late-withdraws are meant to be for-cause withdraws, used for emergencies—a death in the family, a change of circumstance. Technically, it requires documentation and agreement from the professor."

I chewed on my bottom lip, my stomach and heart bouncing around my torso as though my hips had provided a trampoline.

"But I've done a late-withdraw before without this kind of requirement."

"I know most professors in the engineering department don't impose the rule, but it's meant to provide a mechanism for students to withdraw from a class free of penalty when there is a significant event interfering with the student's ability to complete the course. Whether to enforce the policy or not is left to the discretion of the professor."

I sighed, dread rising up to meet me as I sunk into a chair. "So, what do I do? What are my options?"

Professor Cartwright also sighed and I could almost picture her expression of frustration. "These arts and humanities types . . . I've never had one of my engineering students go through this before. But, from what I understand, you have three options: you can take an F in the course, or you can rejoin the class and try to catch up, or you can speak to Professor Kroft and get him to sign off on the late-withdraw."

The sensation of dread spread, cold despair and wretchedness winding its way around my lungs and squeezing.

"Ugh," I said before I could catch myself, because none of those options sounded appealing.

Professor Cartwright waited a beat longer, and then asked, "So, what do you want to do?"

I quickly debated my options, immediately dismissing her proposal to speak with him and obtain his signoff for the late-withdraw. I didn't want to do that. I didn't want to be alone with him or ask him for anything. Plus, clearly, for some bizarre reason only he and his bowties understood, he didn't want me to drop the course.

Because he is a passionless and heartless sadist who lives to make me, and probably countless others, wretched.

The image and associated sensations of him pressing me against the door to his office, touching, and kissing me flashed into memory. Abruptly, I was hot.

Well . . . maybe not passionless.

Moving on.

I dismissed her other idea, that I could try to rejoin the class and hope he'd opt to ignore me, as he'd done before. I refused to be ignored. I deserved better.

It was my desire for respect, control of my own destiny, and the sensibilities of my tender heart that ultimately made the decision.

"I guess I'll take the F." My voice cracked with misery, because I was a good student. An F wouldn't decimate my GPA, but it would make an ugly dent.

My advisor sighed again. "Anna . . . what's going on? I know you. The lowest grade on your transcript is a B. Are you sure you don't want to talk to him? Try to work something out?"

I shook my head before she'd finished speaking. "No. I'll take the F."

"Do you want me to talk to him?"

"No," I blurted, then closed my eyes with remorse. Gathering a deep, calming breath, I tempered my tone. "I'm sorry.

No. Please don't. I . . . he's right. I have no good reason the drop the course. Therefore, I should take the F. I deserve the F."

She made a gruff sound of dissatisfaction, but relented. "Okay. Fine. I'll enter it into the system. But I'll also make a note on your transcript explaining the situation and my disagreement with the outcome."

"You don't have to do that."

"You have one year left, Anna. I hope this debacle isn't a sign of things to come."

"No. Not at all," I promised. "I swear, I just—I should have taken the summer off. I made a mistake. I shouldn't have enrolled in the course."

I shouldn't have enrolled in the course . . .

Truer words had never been spoken.

* * *

Luca sent me an email.

I stumbled across it after two nights of (mostly) restless sleep. Finding an email on my phone from Luca Kroft at 6:14 a.m.—before coffee, before a shower, before moving more than the ten steps required to carry me to where my laptop sat on my desk—was an incredibly effective way to become fully awake.

Tingly, spiky flares of self-consciousness erupted all over my body. I straightened. My breath came short. Heat spread both upward—circling my throat, over my cheeks—and downward to the pit of my stomach.

It sat unread in my inbox, black and bold, with the subject line *Russian Lit*

I felt caught. Found out. Discovered.

Which was ridiculous, since I was alone in my apartment

and he had no power over me. I'd effectively taken his power away when I accepted the F.

I stared at the subject line. Then I stared at it some more. Then I closed my laptop, crossed to the kitchen, made coffee, and took a shower. Dressing quickly, I selected a travel mug, and filled it. I grabbed my keys, phone, and earbuds, and left my apartment.

It may sound silly (all right, it was silly) but I didn't want to open his email in my apartment. It felt like inviting him in, providing the specter of him space to hover. I didn't want Luca—or his sexy ghost—invading my safe place.

A full hundred yards beyond the entrance to the weaving jogging and nature trail around my apartment complex, I claimed a bench, took a large swig of coffee, and opened my email.

Russian Lit

He'd sent it late last night, after midnight. For some reason, this discovery filled me with renewed tingly and spiky self-consciousness—which felt less unwieldy now I was outside. Even so, I folded one arm over my middle, crossed my legs, and gritted my teeth in preparation.

Gathering a bracing breath and ignoring the galloping of my heart, I opened the email.

Dear Anna,

Cartwright stated that you've opted to take an F in Classical Russian Literature. This is a mistake. You held the highest grade prior to your withdrawal. Reconsider. You'll be provided notes for the last two weeks and you may take the skipped weekly assessments. Contact the class TA and she'll administer them at a time of your choosing.

-LK

I read it and reread it. And then read it again a few more times, picking apart every word, word choice, word placement.

What struck me the most was what he'd omitted.

He'd omitted himself.

I'd read a research article in my Intro to Psychology class during my freshman year, discussing the power dynamics of emails. The use of *I, me,* and *my* were associated with a weaker position—usually an employee writing to his or her boss. Whereas, the lack of these pronouns within an email was associated with the individual in power, control.

Luca had omitted all personal and possessive pronouns referring to himself: *I, me, my.* Furthermore, at the end of the message, he'd given me only his initials.

This realization pissed me off. Like . . . SERIOUSLY PISSED ME OFF.

Even now, he was giving me nothing of himself, holding me beyond arms-length, and pushing me into a box labeled *ignore.*

Been there. Done that. Not going back for the T-shirt.

Floating high on my fog of irrational anger, I typed a quick response:

Professor Kroft,
  No, thank you.
  -AIH

Using the middle finger of my right hand, I flicked off the screen of my phone—and therefore, the impervious Luca

Kroft in his superior and sexy bowties and luscious leather pants, wherever he sat high and mighty, perfect and brilliant and untouchable—and hit send. Feeling the rightness of my hasty and haughty response, I decided to use the adrenaline flowing through my veins to fuel a long walk.

As a means of distraction, I listened to my angry music playlist and power-walked like a boss for over an hour. In a fit of insanity, I sprinted for the last five minutes, wanting my pulse to quicken for some purpose other than the thought or sight of Luca Kroft.

Satisfied and spent, I climbed the stairs two at a time to my apartment and rinsed off in the shower before dressing for the day. Work had me scheduled for an evening shift, but I had until 4:00 p.m. all to myself.

And this was a good thing, because I wanted to crack the spines of my fall semester textbooks and browse the first few chapters before the start of the school year.

Absentmindedly, I flipped open my laptop, intent on messaging Emily to see if she had time to study, and that's when I saw it.

Luca had responded. He'd responded just ten minutes after I'd sent my reply.

Except he hadn't hit reply. He'd sent a new message, with a new subject line: *We need to talk.*

I didn't open the email. I didn't need to. The email preview showed me the entirety of his message, which other than a phone number—presumably his—was blank.

* * *

An albatross.

That's what he was.

Or rather, the thought of him was an albatross, hanging

around my neck. I couldn't see past the feathers and bulk of Luca Kroft, clouding my vision and making concentration impossible.

I stumbled, tripping over my feet, on my way to hand over the check to my last table of the evening. I didn't fall, but the almost falling was enough to have me biting back a curse.

Obviously, I hadn't called Luca. I wasn't going to call him. I was going to ignore his imperative. But the fact that he'd made it at all unsettled me.

What could he possibly want to talk about? He ignored me for weeks, I'd made a fool of myself over a B on a paper, we'd kissed, he told me to leave, I dropped the course—end of story.

Leaving the check with the table and assurances that they didn't need to hurry, I left the main dining room and traversed the galley to the break room. It was mostly empty as the night was still relatively young for a Friday. As I'd taken the first evening shift, beginning at four and ending at nine, I would be one of the first to leave once I finished rolling my silverware quota.

I'd just untied my apron when my boss found me. "Ah! Anna, there you are."

I looked up from the stack of black cloth napkins. The big man was hovering in the entranceway, a weird look on his face.

"What's up? What's wrong?"

"You have a new table, number forty-four."

I wrinkled my nose at this news. "What? Now? It's almost nine."

"Yeah, the guy asked for you specifically. You know usually I'd just tell him you're not here, but it's one of the museum's patron families." His frown intensified with an unspoken apology. "How about if you take this table, I'll have someone else finish up your silverware?"

I reached for my apron to re-tie it. "It's fine. I don't mind."

I brushed past him on the way out and hurriedly glanced at the table where I'd left the check. They'd already left, so I took a moment to gather their payment, then navigated the still-busy restaurant. Table forty-four was a booth with high seatbacks at the edge of the restaurant, hidden away and typically reserved for romantic twosomes wanting quiet and privacy.

Therefore, I didn't see him until I drew even with the table. But when I did, when I saw it was him and that he was alone, I stopped.

Luca.

I stopped and I stared, unconsciously holding my breath. To breathe was to admit I could not pause and rewind my reality, I could not undo the seeing of him.

He said nothing, instead opting to openly study me in his steady way.

When I could take no more of his detached perusal, I blurted, "What are you doing here?"

"Eating. Hopefully." His icy irises felt like hooks, digging into some unseen part of myself and holding me hostage.

"You can't—" I needed to swallow before I could continue. "You can't come here, just show up. This is where I work."

"Why not? You showed up where I work." He sounded so entirely reasonable, but with an edge of something else. Something I couldn't place, but had the fine hairs on the back of my neck raising in warning.

"Because I was your student," I seethed through clenched teeth.

"And now I'm your customer."

"Luca."

"Anna."

My lashes fluttered, as though he'd blown dust into my eyes. Magical, heart-wrenching, alluring man-dust. I both hated and adored the way he said my name: softly, reverently, beseechingly. It made me breathless and warm, flustered and absorbed. Absorbed in him. *By him.* Only him.

We stared at each other and the albatross around my neck grew heavier, but in the wrong direction. Instead of weighing me down, it tugged me forward, toward Luca. I stumbled a step closer, my thighs touching the edge of the table.

"Fine. What do you want?" I wanted to sound cold, aloof, but instead the words arrived as a shaky whisper. I couldn't stop staring at his lips.

I've kissed those.

The thought inspired a wave of longing, a spike of regret, a twist of desire—each sharper and more disorienting than the last.

He didn't respond, waiting until I returned my gaze to his. What I saw, the force and focus of his stare, made me swallow and stiffen.

Instinctively, I edged away.

Luca reached out and grabbed my wrist, circling it with his large hand. The unexpected contact halted my backward momentum.

"Anna," he said, arresting me, tugging me back to the table. "When are you finished tonight? When can you leave?"

I thought about lying, but I couldn't. Not when he was gazing at me, his thumb rubbing a slow circle on the inside of my wrist, and his voice echoing the tenderness of his touch.

I had to clear my throat before I could form words. "You're my only table. When you leave, I can leave."

His stare turned searching. Actually, *probing* was more accurate. I watched him, transfixed as his eyes narrowed slightly, the side of his jaw and temple ticked belying his frustration, or resolve, or both. Eventually, he nodded once, releasing my wrist.

"Order a bottle of Louis Roederer Cristal Brut." Luca reached into his pocket and withdrew his wallet, finding several bills. "Meet me in the patron parking lot. We'll ride together."

"I'm not . . ." I began but stalled, frowning at the five one-hundred dollar bills he'd pressed into my palm, but unable to make sense of them. "There's nothing to say," I finally managed, shaking my head at the wad of cash. "I have nothing to say to you."

"Then you'll listen."

"But—"

"Anna." My name a caress, he effectively killed the objection on the tip of my tongue. Nothing about him was soft except how he said my name.

Why does this man make me so weak? Why?

. . . because he's brilliant and fascinating and—against all odds and laws of nature—looks amazing in leather pants.

Obviously.

Not waiting for me to respond, he stood from the booth, once more reaching for my wrist and tugging me closer. Again, before I could comprehend what was happening, Luca bent and brushed a gentle kiss over my mouth. I sucked in a shocked breath, too stiff and hot with surprise to move.

He lingered, nipping my bottom lip and tasting it with his tongue at the last minute, like it was compulsory, like he couldn't help himself.

I swayed forward as he released me. He turned before I could inspect his eyes, striding unhurriedly to the exit.

PART 10

** ANNA **

I met Luca in the parking lot, but didn't know how to feel about . . . anything.

Logicaling (of note, *logicaling* is not a real word, kids) my way through things was completely out of the question. Though I didn't know how to feel, I also felt too much.

I held myself back, stopping six feet from where he sat on his motorcycle, watching me silently as I approached holding his bottle of champagne.

Luca studied me with outward dispassion for a long moment, and then offered me a helmet. "Put it on."

I lifted an eyebrow at the helmet, then at him. "No, thank you. I'll drive my car. Where do you want me to put this?" I held up the bottle.

"Keep it." Luca nodded once, apparently unfazed, and secured the helmet to the back of his motorcycle. "Follow me."

I wanted to ask, *Follow you where?* but I said nothing. This was likely because I was muddled, flustered by the sight of him and the unexpected kiss in the restaurant. My blood was still pumping hot and thick through my veins at the memory of him nipping and tasting my bottom lip.

If I boldly walked over to him, wrapped my arms around his neck, and bit his lip in a similar fashion . . . what would he do?

Before I could take any action, he revved his motorcycle to life. I jumped inelegantly, squeaking at the unexpected sound—only unexpected because my brain had been distracted with thoughts of boldly kissing him.

He glanced at me questioningly, as though to ask, *Changed your mind?* about the motorcycle ride.

I shook my head quickly and turned, jogging to my car two lanes over and arriving out of breath. After fumbling and fighting with my keys and discarding the champagne to my back seat, I was soon out of the employee lot.

I followed him off the museum grounds to the main thoroughfare, on the highway, off the downtown exit, left on Park Street, and into a parking garage for one of the high-rises overlooking the park and adjacent to the river.

I drove on autopilot, following without focusing too much on where we were going, where he was leading me. I was preoccupied.

We've kissed. Two times now. And I enjoyed it, a lot. I am no longer his student. He is no longer my professor. And he gave you an F for dropping his class. Do we like him? . . . I don't know. But we've kissed.

Unfortunately, I'd made it no further than these sentiments. They were a continuous loop in my brain even as Luca motioned for me to take a parking spot by the elevator—which I did—while he parked his bike behind a Mercedes adjacent to my car.

Luca opened my door just as I unbuckled my seatbelt, reaching in and holding my hand with his gloved fingers to help me stand. Saying nothing, he tugged me forward, shutting the door, and lead me to the elevator.

I swallowed tightly, glancing at his large hand holding mine, his encased in black leather.

What was happening? I wanted to ask. *What were we doing?*

Instead, I managed, "Do you live here?"

His eyes flickered to me, holding mine just briefly before moving back to the elevator. "My family has a place in the building. It's not mine."

I nodded, trying to project an outward air of nonchalance to disguise my inner turmoil.

In unison, we stepped onto the elevator. He released my hand, pressed a button for the forty-seventh floor, and scanned a card at the panel.

On instinct, I yawned as the pressure built in my ears.

"The pressure," I murmured.

"Pardon?" I felt his gaze move back to me, studying my profile.

I motioned to my head, explaining, "The pressure, from the rapid ascent. I'm not tired, even though I'm yawning."

His eyebrows inched upward, but he said nothing. Just looked at me. He looked at me like I was the weird one in this elevator. This banal *looking* made my neck itch beneath the starched collar of my work shirt.

"I'm not the weird one," I blurted, frowning at his non-expression. "If one of us is the weird one, it's you."

The side of his mouth tugged upward at the same time he cocked a single eyebrow. "I'm the weird one?"

"Yep. You're the weird one." I nodded at my own words, facing the elevator panel and not looking at Luca. "I'm the normal one."

He huffed what sounded like an incredulous laugh. "Yes.

95

Very normal. You chose to drop a class and take an F instead of finishing with an A."

My mouth fell open just as the elevator *dinged*, announcing our arrival. Before I could speak, Luca grabbed my hand again and pulled me after him into the dark hallway, leading me three steps inside before releasing my fingers.

"Hey," I protested when I found my voice. "What was I supposed to do?"

I listened as his footsteps echoed away from me. A light switched on above us, illuminating the fact that we weren't in a hallway at all. We were in a large foyer of what appeared to be a massive apartment.

I took a moment to get my bearings, searching the space. The décor and architecture were extremely modern. Surrounded by grays and whites and natural wood on all sides, paintings and sculptures hung on the walls. A gigantic living room lay just beyond where Luca stood with a long bar off to one side. A floor-to-ceiling window spanned the entire length and overlooked the city and park beyond.

I refocused my attention on him just as he turned and sauntered—yes, sauntered—into the living area and to the bar. "Do you want something to drink?"

The polished, understated yet immense lavishness of my surroundings made me feel small and shabby in comparison.

Meanwhile, Luca—who was tugging off his gloves—looked . . . at home.

If he was trying to intimidate me with his slow, sensual glove removal and the *immense lavishness*, it wouldn't work. Yes, I felt shabby and small, but that's okay. I was shabby and small. There's nothing wrong with being shabby and small. Hobbits are shabby and small and look how badass they are.

Plus, second breakfasts for the win.

Lifting my chin and dropping my bag by the door, I

followed his footsteps into the living room and to the bar. "Yes. I'll have a Shirley Temple—"

He made a scoffing sound.

The sound ended abruptly as I finished, "—with vodka."

His eyes darted to mine as he placed his gloves on the bar. "Then it's not a Shirley Temple."

"I don't care what you call it as long as you make it." I shrugged, mentally high-fiving myself for sounding so calm and not doofus-like. Riding the wave of verbal success, I asked, "Why are we here?"

"We need to talk." He pulled out a can of 7 Up, a bottle of Zyr, and set to mixing my drink.

"I already told you in the restaurant, I have nothing to say to you."

"You said I was withholding myself from you, you said I give you nothing."

I flinched, my breath catching and my heart twisting at the memory. Unable to speak as Luca finished preparing our drinks, I sat numbly on a barstool and clutched my hands together on my lap.

I hadn't expected him to be so direct.

"I can understand now why that upset you," he noted simply, walking around the bar to take the stool next to mine. He faced me, his gaze traveling down and then up my body in a way that felt meaningful, then added in a roughened tone, "I don't like it when you withhold yourself from me. You shouldn't have dropped the class."

Struggling to keep hold of my wits and anger, I fought a rising heat caused by his blatant once-over of my form and by his blunt words, but my voice cracked tellingly as I asked, "Again, what was I supposed to do?"

He tilted his head to the side, glaring at me, his elbow

resting on the bar, the back of his hand brushing against his lips. "I don't like it when you leave."

"Are you talking about after the . . . kiss? You told me to go."

"I didn't like it."

I glanced at the ceiling, growling, then returned my scowl to his granite expression. "You ignore me. You k-kiss me. You tell me to leave. And now you tell me you don't like it when I leave. What do you want from me, Luca?"

Crap. I hated that I stumbled over the word *kiss.* But saying it to him or discussing what we'd done, even though it made no logical sense, felt forbidden somehow.

"Finish the semester." Leaning slightly forward, he placed his palm on the bar between us. "Finish what you started. For once."

"You don't know anything about me." I endeavored to keep my temper out of my tone because his words made me irrationally angry. "I finish what I start, *thankyouverymuch.*"

"Really?"

"Yes. I'll have you know I've completed over seventeen jigsaw puzzles just this year and I've never DNF-ed a book, though sorely I've been tempted."

"Oh. I see. You just don't follow through with things that are difficult."

I winced, clutching my heart. "Wow. Wow . . . wow. And ouch."

Luca's gaze dropped to the carpet and he sighed, which sounded frustrated.

"You're kind of mean," I said to the room, and then nodded to myself. "But I guess I already knew that."

He cleared his throat and returned his attention to me, the lines of his face hard, unyielding. "Come back." It was a demand.

"No."

"You want to be there. You love it."

"How would you know? You never look at me." I picked up my not-Shirley Temple and took a sip. It was strong, but it also tasted like bravery.

"I see you, Anna." His voice lowered an octave, as though he were endeavoring to control his temper; his hand on the bar inched closer. "It's impossible not to see you."

"Yeah, well, then you're good at pretending I'm invisible." I gulped my drink.

He waited a beat, inspecting me, before speaking again in a hushed tone. "If I looked at you, if I called on you, if I allowed myself to debate with you during class, I would never speak to anyone else."

"So you ignore me." I licked my lips, tasting the sweet soda and grenadine on my lips, turning my gaze to his.

His attention was on my mouth. "Yes. For your benefit as well as mine."

"How is you ignoring me beneficial *to me*? I'd really like to know."

He paused, his stare sharpening into a glare. "You're very young."

"Thank you . . . ?"

Luca's eyes lifted to mine. "You're impetuous."

"Enough with the compliments, Luca. I'm blushing," I deadpanned through clenched teeth, the ball of frustration in my chest ballooning to near critical size.

"I'm your professor—"

"*Were* my professor. Past tense."

"I never should have kissed you."

"Which time?" I seethed, his statement a punch in the stomach.

Luca nodded, as though accepting the veracity of my

anger. "It was inappropriate and wrong, and I'm . . ." Luca gathered a deep breath, giving me the impression he was preparing to speak rehearsed words, "I apologize for my inappropriate behavior. If you want to drop the class, I will sign off. If you want to report me to my Department Chair, I fully support your decision."

In a fit of fury-fueled insanity, I spat, "Report you for what? Kissing me? In case you're confused about where I stood on the subject of us kissing, I was all for it."

The muscle at his jaw jumped, and he continued with his prepared speech as though I hadn't spoken, "Despite my regrettable actions, I take my role as your professor seriously. You deserve an impartial teacher, and I have failed you. But I could not let you go. . ." He paused to swallow, giving me the sense he needed a second before finishing his thought. "I could not let you drop the class when it is I who am to blame."

I tried to keep up with him, and I was certain I missed most of the nuance behind his words. Because, ultimately, all my yearning heart heard was: *I regret kissing you, kissing you was wrong.* Maybe with a side of, *You're too young for me,* and *Let's keep things professional from now on.*

And now I understood what it was to feel truly wretched.

Glaring at him, I lifted my chin. "I don't care what you say, I don't regret anything. You can't take blame for something I refuse to feel upset about. And I think you're a jerk for telling me you regret it. A jerk and a coward."

Unexpectedly, the side of his mouth tugged upward, and I didn't think it was my imagination when he swayed forward a scant inch.

But his eyes were seasoned with sadness as he whispered, "Wait for your Pierre, Natasha."

My planned volley of sarcasm died in my throat, strangled by his comparison. I could only stare at him.

That's not entirely true. I could only blink and stare at him, my mouth working to no purpose, because if he considered me to be Natasha, then Luca was . . .

He thinks he's Andrei.

PART 11

** ANNA **

"*. . .* S end you the remainder of the assignments. As stated in my email, the TA can administer missed coursework . . ."

I frowned at him, at the pleasing cadence of his voice, at his gorgeous face. I hadn't been listening. My brain was stuck in the past. Specifically, stuck on his words from moments ago, when he'd called me Natasha.

Because, how could I not fixate on the comparison?

Natasha, lovely, lively, spirited Natasha.

Naïve Natasha, ruled by her emotions.

Disloyal Natasha, easily seduced by the scoundrel—shoot! What's that guy's name?

Repentant Natasha, but not repentant enough for Andrei.

She was never enough for Andrei, doomed to failure from the start.

I decided I disliked his analogy.

I hated it.

Meanwhile, Luca was still talking.

" . . . don't need to come into class, if you have no desire to attend. But I hope you—"

"I resent the comparison," I announced. Loudly. Smacking the bar with my palm.

Luca pressed his lips into a thin line, his jaw ticking, his gaze growing hooded. "Anna—"

"Don't say my name. No more saying my name!" I stood and marched to the door. I heard his muted footfalls on the carpet as he trailed me.

"Where are you going?"

"I'm going home," I grumbled, retrieving my bag from the floor and pressing the elevator call button. I was so done with him.

Stick a fork in this BS.

"Then I'll see you in class."

I scoffed, gritting my teeth as I turned to face him. "Yeah. Sure. Fine. See you in class, Professor Kroft. Sounds good, Professor Kroft." I jabbed the call button again. "Whatever you say, *Professor Kroft.*"

Luca shoved his fine fingers in his pants pockets and glowered at me—one eyebrow slightly higher than the other —as though my sarcastic outburst had just proved his point: immature Natasha and sophisticated Andrei never belonged together.

Doomed.

This was not the first time he'd made me feel like less. Like I wasn't worthy of . . . him. His time. Rationally, I knew this feeling was dissonant with the truth. He'd gone out of his way to contact me, keep me in his class. As a teacher, he was doing his due diligence.

As a man, he'd kissed me for Frodo's sake! TWICE!

And yet, as much as I recognized he was an excellent teacher, a brilliant professor, and gifted scholar, I didn't like him—the man—very much. Because, as a man—after the kisses were over—I'd felt small and shabby.

And not in a badass Hobbit way either.

"Anna—"

"You know," I rounded on him, holding a hand up between us, "just stop. Stop. I get it. I do. You're attracted to me, or you were—whatever—and I'm your student, or I was. But I'm also young, and not just age-wise. I'm young in a perpetually immature, goofy-person way. Which means I'm 'not your kind of nice.' Even if we were the same age, or if I were older than you, I'd *still* be 'not your kind of nice.'"

I watched him gather a deep breath, watched as his eyes moved between mine and his lips parted as though he wanted to contradict. But he didn't. He swallowed and said nothing.

I didn't expect him to speak. I knew he wasn't my kind of nice either. How could I judge him for sharing the same thoughts? I couldn't.

We didn't fit. We didn't make sense. We never would.

Dooooooomed!

The elevator dinged, announcing its arrival. I tore my gaze from his and stepped onto the lift, my heart heavy as I pressed the button for the parking garage.

Luca placed his hand on the space where the door disappeared into the wall, keeping it from sliding shut. "Will I see you in class?" he asked quietly, his tone tight and refrained.

I gave him a small, humorless smile. "How about this. I'll make you a deal. I'll re-enroll if you promise to call on me during class once a week."

I didn't expect him to agree. I expected him to scoff, to lift an indifferent eyebrow and dismiss me without a word. I'd even begun digging in my bag, searching for my keys, because I considered the matter settled.

"Fine. Deal," he said, removing his hand from the doorway.

My head snapped up and I gaped at him, shocked. "Deal?"

"Deal." He nodded once, his lips a grim line, his serious eyes more somber than I'd ever seen them.

"But—"

"See you Monday," he said gruffly.

Then the door closed.

The elevator descended.

I was caught, ensnared in a trap of my own design.

PART 12

** LUCA **

*M*y older sister lived in our father's building. She received a monthly stipend, deposited into her personal bank account automatically, as recompense of her *efforts on behalf of the family*.

She accompanied our father on trips, served as a hostess for his parties, and shelved her own interests—personal and professional—in favor of his whims.

Dominika didn't complain. Nor did she appear to be unhappy with the arrangement.

She'd emerged from what our father called *the rebellious phase*, a period during which his children were determined to live their life outside of his influence, make their own decisions, and thus relentlessly dissatisfy him.

I was still in my rebellious phase.

If his opinion wasn't consulted, even successes were a disappointment. Scholarships, degrees, awards, grants—all meaningless.

Ultimately, however, and despite my fiercest efforts, Sergey Kroft's influence was impossible to escape. He'd made certain of that.

"Dr. Kroft," Dr. McGovern stood as I entered his office; he extended a hand if not a genuine smile. "Please come in, sit."

I walked to a new set of leather club chairs and took the one closest to the door. The Persian rug was new, as were the shelves lining both walls, the conference table, the stained glass lamps, and the desk. My attention idled on what appeared to be a gold- plated stapler next to a futuristic looking conferencing telephone.

The forthcoming discussion was certain to be uncomfortable, now even more so with evidence of my father's influence infiltrating every corner, and this was precisely why I hadn't wanted to bring Anna into this world, my father's world.

"What do you need?" The head of my department rested in his wingback desk chair, tepid smile in place.

"An impartial mediator is needed for a student in the summer session." Impatience to have this exchange over imbued my tone with clipped efficiency.

Outcome certain, I saw no use delaying inexorable unpleasantness.

If circumstances had been different, if I'd earned my place as a tenured professor, if I—and Dr. McGovern—were free of Sergey Kroft's influence, then I would be holding a resignation letter. No one would ever know that the captivating Anna I. Harris had been my reason and I would breathe easier.

Reality held us both hostage, to a point.

Dr. McGovern tugged on the hidden tray holding his keyboard and moved his attention to the new flat screen monitor on his desk. "Why do you need the mediator?"

"Compromised impartiality."

"Why?"

"I hope to become involved with the student."

And there it was.

Dr. McGovern ceased typing. His stare slid from the monitor to mine, and held. Previous traces of forced friendliness now gone, a flinty expression emerged. This, at last, was sincere.

When I'd met Dr. McGovern years ago, a CRT monitor sat on his pressed wood desk. The office had been shabbily decorated in postmodern avocado greens, peeling vinyl chairs that smelled like cigarettes, and shag carpet, presumably bequeathed from one Department Chair to the next since the 1960's.

"Please don't take this the wrong way. . ."

Bracing for the impressive pomposity of the exceptionally hypocritical, I inclined my head for the Department Chair to continue.

"I imagine it must be difficult for you, not knowing if your position, your tenue has been earned, or if it was a consequence of your family's generosity to this great institution."

He paused, and we shared what I suspected was meant to be a meaningful look, one that left me in no doubt of his thoughts on the matter.

"If you were any other young faculty member—an adjunct, or an assistant professor—you would be dismissed for this. This is a small world we live in and your credibility would be destroyed."

He paused, as though to *let that sink in*, before continuing philosophically, "And if you were any other *tenured* faculty member, you'd be old enough to know better. Or, you'd be dismissed, forced to quietly retire. Let me be clear, I would force you out. I do not tolerate harassment of my students, the preying upon of young people by those in authority." His gaze dropped to the gold stapler I'd noticed earlier. "But we both know you are not any other professor."

Absolute power corrupts absolutely. And so does money.

Giving him nothing—no reaction, no words of explanation—I leaned my elbow on the arm of the club chair and covered my mouth with a hand. I waited.

Dr. McGovern also waited, but he'd be waiting indefinitely if his expectations included an impassioned defense, or contrition. I wasn't the first professor to become involved with a student in our department—nor would I be the last—and therefore, his righteous speech was little more than sanctimonious blather.

Notwithstanding the bloated opinions of the sycophant across from me, *I* was discontented with myself. My weakness disappointed me. But I'd never confess as much to him.

"Well?" The older man leaned backward, turning his hands palm up, apparently dissatisfied with my lack of comment.

I scratched my cheek. "Would you like a resignation letter?"

He considered me, ubiquitous contempt painting the man a shade of green that would have complemented the office's previous décor. "Of course not."

"Then, a mediator."

Dr. McGovern nodded once, his thin lips now a thinner line, the two bits of flesh pressed together somehow less than each separately. "Fine. If you have no respect for the tenets of this institution, a mediator will be arranged."

My goal accomplished, I stood. "How soon?"

He threw a hand in the air. "Next week," he blustered,

exasperated, as though he'd been the one disenfranchised and preyed upon.

Next week.

I nodded, turned, and left.

One week.

I sailed down the hall, past the department secretary, not pausing to check my messages.

I wasn't proud of my decisions where Anna was concerned. But for once in my life, pride seemed to matter not at all.

I wanted Anna.

I wanted to be with her, even if I wasn't yet free to be with her *fully.*

If she is willing, this will have to be enough.

Yes, Anna was beautiful—I considered her the most beautiful woman I'd ever known—but it was her words that preoccupied me, unbearably brief glimpses into an exquisite soul. The email she'd sent in February, her responses to discussion test questions, the essay she'd written before dropping the class.

Each time we were alone, a surge of intrinsic rightness overwhelmed caution, circumspection eclipsed by an agonizing curiosity. I needed to *know* her. We'd barely touched, but these encounters—things left unsaid, actions untaken—haunted me.

My life split in two: before and after; the possibility of she, of hope and wonder; and then everything else.

. .

I didn't deserve her, not yet. Not until my book was finished and published. Not until I'd secured enough in grant funding to be independent of the endowment my father had made in my name. Not until I'd succeeded in fully supporting myself, until I could offer her a life free of Sergey Kroft's influence.

Then I'd be able to offer myself to her completely.

It might take months, or years. But it would be worth it.

For now, for this first step, I could wait one more week. Just one week. I could force circumspection.

For one week.

PART 13

** ANNA **

"*T*he themes include infidelity, jealousy, hypocrisy, faith, family, marriage, and society. *Anna Karenina* is considered to be Tolstoy's first true novel as well as one of the greatest novels of all time . . ."

I didn't roll my eyes, but if I'd been an eye-roller I definitely would have.

Anna Karenina was my least favorite of Tolstoy's works. Every character was a stereotype, a flat caricature lacking in depth, the only purpose, to play out scenarios in order to highlight Tolstoy's precious themes.

The saint.

The sinner.

The ingénue.

The selfless hero.

The fallen woman.

Blarg and gag.

"What was Anna's greatest mistake?" Luca asked the class, his eyes skimming over the lecture hall.

It was Friday. I'd returned to class on Monday, easily

explaining away my absence to Taylor and other classmates as a personal emergency.

On Monday, I'd raised my hand every time he posed a question. He never called on me.

On Wednesday, I lifted my arm about half the time. Same result.

Today, I tried three times and then gave up.

Not only had Luca never called on me, he hadn't looked at me all week. He hadn't made any sign that I was anything other than invisible.

Just like old times.

At present, I was sketching a possible design for my cosplay costume and not really paying attention to the discussion or the lecture. I'd had just about as much as I could take of watching him interact with other students, watching how they engaged and became excited, watching how he'd hold them captive in the palm of his hand.

That would never be me, and that was okay.

Moving on.

"Anna . . ." Luca's voice said from somewhere at the front of the lecture hall, and I completely zoned out.

I'd decided I'd be Tank Girl for Comic-Con. The outfit would be a challenge, but I'd found an online tutorial for making armor out of PVP foam and Mod Podge. Mod Podge was basically magic in a bottle for crafters.

Taylor nudged me with her elbow, yanking my attention away from the sketch. I frowned at her, and she stared back with wide eyes, indicating with her head toward the front of the lecture hall.

Confused, I glanced in the direction she indicated and found Luca leaning against the long table at the front, looking at me.

A shock of surprise and awareness slapped me across the face, and I sat straighter in my seat.

"Ms. Harris, do you need me to repeat the question?"

I nodded. "Yes, please."

Luca's tone was even as he asked, "What was Anna's greatest mistake?"

Without thinking too much about it, I responded, "Allowing others to define her worth rather than having a strong sense of self."

Luca's stare turned fuzzy for a beat as he processed my response, and confusion knit his eyebrows. "You don't think her greatest mistake was giving in to Vronsky? Leaving her husband, Alexej Karenin?"

"No. She didn't belong with Karenin. She did the right thing by leaving him."

He crossed his arms over his chest, his frown deepening, and lifted his chin toward me. "Please explain."

I knew this tactic. I'd watched Luca employ this one hundred times during class, always when he disagreed with a student and was preparing a counterargument. He'd listen to their thoughts and ideas—which were typically ill-formed and lacking conviction—and then he'd poke holes in it until the student conceded, adding another heart-mind combo to his vast collection.

Gathering a deep breath, I shifted my eyes to the wipe board behind him; I couldn't look at him and his distracting sexy bowtie if I was going to *actually* debate my point.

"Anna—who is charismatic, charming, vivacious, gorgeous, intelligent, and extremely vain—marries Karenin—a boring, rigid senior government official who she finds unattractive . . .".," I paused for dramatic effect, then added, "Probably because he's boring."

A short whisper of laughter rumbled over the class, cut

even shorter by Luca casting his unimpressed gaze over the students.

Not waiting for him to rebuke me, I continued, "Anna didn't belong with Karenin. Leaving him was the right thing to do, for both of them. Falling in love with Vronsky made sense, as he was more her speed."

"You didn't find him shallow?"

"Of course I did," I responded immediately. "He was shallow, and vain, and pretentious. I would never date him, but he was perfect for her. Plus, Vronsky was also passionately in love with Anna. And he was loyal to Anna throughout the entirety of the book, even when others shun her, even when she starts boiling bunnies."

"And yet, Anna *is* shunned by society, rebuffed at the theater for her sins."

"Yes. Exactly. She is shunned. And so what? If she'd had a stronger sense of herself, then the shunning and rebuffing would hold little concern for her. If you know who you are, rejection matters very little. It says more about the small-mindedness of the person who is doing the rejecting than it does about you."

This last sentence rang through the air for a good twenty seconds after I said it. Though there was no echo, it echoed.

It resonated.

At least, it resonated with me. It bounced around my brain and felt so very, very, very correct.

The class remained still and quiet, apparently lost to their own thoughts. Meanwhile, Luca and I stared at each other, his frown easing as he—also still and quiet—studied me.

Eventually, he gathered a deep breath and countered thoughtfully, "But what of the parallel between Vronsky's horse and his treatment of Anna?"

"Anna is not a horse. On behalf of women everywhere, I

object to Tolstoy's attempt to draw a parallel between a farm animal and a woman. Again, it speaks volumes about Tolstoy, but I digress. If Anna based her worth on how badass and awesome she was, rather than the opinions of those who rejected her, then she would have lived a long, happy life with her daughter and smokin' hot lover, Vronsky. Instead, she throws herself in front of a train, just because she isn't invited to a party."

"People cannot dwell or thrive in isolation."

"She wasn't isolated. She had peasants," I said with a grin. "She should have befriended the peasants. Peasants are awesome and throw great parties."

Another rumble of laughter rippled through the lecture hall and, though Luca's eyebrows told me he was still frowning, his mouth curved into a betraying smile.

"And what of pride?" he asked softly. "What of a place in society? In one's own family?"

I flicked my wrist with a dismissive gesture. "Pride is just another word for insecurity and fear—again, having no strong sense of self or worth. If pride is the driving force behind your decisions, then your life is going to suck." I stopped myself before saying *balls,* as in: *your life is going to suck balls.*

After a long moment, Luca nodded—very slowly at first —his eyes hazy with his own ponderings.

"But . . ." I started, feeling a small twinge of guilt since I'd ignored the point Luca was trying to make in favor of expressing my own perspective. "My answer is, of course, colored by the lens of modern individualist values. Therefore —given the fact that Anna Karenina was written prior to the perspectivism movement of the nineteenth century, and framing the story in Tolstoy's themes on infidelity, vanity, selflessness, and family—I concede that Tolstoy wanted us to believe that Anna's greatest mistake was succumbing to the temptation of Vronsky."

"How magnanimous of you." Luca's smile spread, like he was suppressing a laugh, and I fell head first into his gaze. His eyes were twinkling at me.

I shrugged, an unbidden flush of pleasure heating my neck and cheeks, momentarily forgetting we were not alone. "Well, my middle name *is* benevolent."

"No it's not, it's Iris," he said, then blinked, snapping his mouth shut, visibly startled by his own words.

Clearly, he hadn't meant to say them.

And I hadn't expected him to say them. I stared at him blankly, opening my mouth to no purpose while a heavy silence fell over the class. I felt eyes on me from every direction, moving between my face and his.

Don't look guilty.

Don't. Look. Guilty.

DON'T LOOK GUILTY!

The most difficult thing to do is *not look guilty* when your brain is telling you to not look guilty.

Not difficult, however, making an awkward joke.

"It's true," I blurted. "My cousin used to call me Anna Eyeball."

This earned me a few chuckles, enough that I was able to tear my gaze from his and glance unseeingly at the sketch I'd been drawing. I swallowed thickly, willing my thundering heart to slow.

"Yes, well . . ." Luca said, his voice tight. He cleared his throat and then continued in a steady, instructional tone. "Given that we've established Tolstoy wanted us to believe Anna Karenina's greatest mistake was giving into the temptation of Vronsky, let's take a look at Kitty's path in comparison."

I tucked my chin to my chest and added several pointless lines to my costume sketch, emphatically ignoring the weight of Taylor's probing gaze from my right. It was easy to do, because I was obsessing. And try as I might, I could not stop obsessing over the truth betrayed by Luca's thoughtlessly spoken words.

He'd looked up my middle name.

Let that sink in.

Eventually, the sounds of class dismissing paired with Taylor nudging me again forced my attention away from the sketch on my desk.

Leaning close, she spoke low, so only I could hear. "Don't look, but Professor Kroft is staring at you."

I choked on my immediate reaction—which was to ask, *What is his expression like? Does he look angry? Sad? Plagued by infatuation? Crushed under the weight of unrequited affection?*—and instead managed a weird chuckle. "Don't be ridiculous."

"He is," she whispered on an excited rush. "Well, he's typing on his phone now. But he was staring at you. No, wait —now he's looking up here again."

I stacked and restacked my papers, reaching for my backpack. "Maybe he's looking at you."

"Ha! No. Professor Kroft doesn't know *my* middle name."

"Yes, he does. He knows everyone's middle name. I'm sure it's on the roster."

"It's not. Just initials are on the roster."

I finally looked at her and asked before I could catch myself, "How would you know that?"

She shrugged, grinning. "I'm a TA for the Art History Department. I know what class rosters look like and they only have initials for middle names."

Closing my eyes for a beat, I sighed. Really, I only sighed

because I was stalling. Stalling and deflecting were essential life skills I'd learned at home when my dad would ask me, *You didn't stay up reading all night again, did you?*

Most of the other students had already cleared out, leaving only a few stragglers. It might have been my imagination, but I felt the weight of stares on my face and back. Not wanting to be one of the few loitering, I pulled my backpack to my shoulder and turned for the stairs.

"I have to go."

"Wait, want to grab something to eat?" Taylor jumped from her seat, clutching her computer and bag to her chest.

"I, uh—"

"Come on." She rushed forward, looping her arm with mine. "Don't you want to discuss possible theories of why Professor Kroft made it a point to know your middle name?"

"No. I don't. I really, really don't. I have to go." I shook my head—with feeling—as we climbed the stairs arm in arm, trying not to think about how this would look to Luca from the lecture hall floor.

"Come on, Anna. The way he was looking at you? When he called you magnanimous? Gah!" She pushed the door open to the outside as she whispered excitedly, "I'm not the only one who noticed, it was impossible not to."

I increased the speed of my head shake. "I have plans. I have things to do. I'm already late. I have . . ." I'd pulled out my phone, as though it would give my excuses more credibility, then frowned at the screen.

A notification had just popped up.

I had a new email.

And it was from Luca.

PART 14

"*Y*ou seem weird."

"What?"

Emily poked me with a long stalk of celery. "You seem weird. You seem off."

I sucked in a large breath, held it in my lungs, and returned my attention to the Concrete Structures textbook I'd been perusing. I couldn't recall a single detail about its contents.

"I'm fine," I breathed out.

She poked me again. "No. You've been off for weeks, all summer in fact, but today you're even worse than usual. Something is going on. You're keeping secrets."

I frowned at the textbook, staring at it without seeing the words, and shook my head.

But she was right.

I'd told her nothing of my interactions with Luca and I wondered if withholding this information somehow broke the unwritten best friend code. I didn't think so.

This wasn't anything as banal as me having a crush on my professor. Of course, I *did* have a crush on him. In an odd reversal of societal norms, Luca's external hotness played second fiddle to the sexiness of his brain. Most of the class—both male and female—had a crush on his brain. Fact.

No. The secret I kept from my best friend wasn't the crush.

"Tell me." She poked me once more.

I closed my textbook with a smack. "Fine."

"I knew it." Emily shot up in her chair, jabbing the celery in the air. "I knew it. What happened? It's got to be good if you're this agitated."

"I'm not agitated."

"Yes, darling, you are agitated. You've been missing easy questions on trivia night. My guess is some boy has stolen your heart."

"Why would you think that?" I tried to make a face of denial and failed, more curious for her answer than concerned she'd figured out the truth.

"Because that stone-cold fox hit on you last Tuesday and you were even more oblivious than usual."

"Who?"

"The musician guy? The one who asked if you would sit on his lap?"

This time I successfully made a face. "He wasn't hitting on me."

"Yeah. He was. Pro tip, Anna: if any guy other than Santa Claus asks you to sit on his lap, he's hitting on you. So spill it. Spill your guts. Spill them everywhere."

I frowned, attempting to parse my thoughts. "Okay, first, you have to promise not to tell anyone. And I mean *anyone*. No one can know about this conversation. Ever."

"Oh. Okay. Crap. Fine, I promise. Jeez, who is this guy? A professor?"

...

...

...

...

Shit.

Emily's eyes widened and she inclined her head forward.

I held my hands up. "Wait, just listen—"

"Don't tell me, it's the Russian Lit guy, right? Damn. I guess I need to take this class. Everyone talks about this guy."

"It's not what you think."

"*Puh*-lease. I've seen his picture. You don't have a crush on him?"

"I do, but—"

She waved the rest of my words away with a dismissive flick of her wrist. "I thought something serious was going on with you. I can't believe you fell under his spell."

I made a face. "What do you mean, *under his spell*?"

"Like I told you before you took the class, this guy is the resident sexy professor of infamy. He's famous on campus for being hot and unobtainable. Since he was hired, there's always a story floating around about students—both undergrad and post-grad—throwing themselves at him and being unceremoniously rejected, and then reprimanded and reported for their shenanigans."

"What kind of shenanigans?"

"When I told my friend Darcy—you know, from poly sci? —when I told her you were in his class, she told me a story about a girl last year who waited for him—naked—in his office. He was giving a tour to the foreign language endowment chancellor and . . ." Emily pursed her lips, giving me a meaningful look. "Let's just say it was awkward in every language."

I winced, on behalf of Luca but also on behalf of the girl. "That's terrible."

"Yeah, but not the first or the last time he'll have to deal with naked students or unrequited crushes. I guess I'm surprised you'd be so agitated by the power of a pretty face." She reached for and patted my hand. "But, in your defense, his face is exceptionally pretty."

I absorbed this information, my mind tripping over the words *unobtainable* and *unrequited,* thinking back to Luca's email earlier in the evening.

I hadn't read the message outside the lecture hall. I'd waited until I was away from Taylor and in the safety of my own car, then I devoured it. It had read,

Dear Anna,

There is a matter I need to discuss with you. I'll be in my office after class.

-Luca

"Sorry to burst your bubble."

I blinked at my friend. "What?"

"Your bubble. Your fantasy bubble that had you and this Russian Lit guy moving off the grid and quoting depressing gothic romance to each other." Emily grinned at me teasingly.

Before I could stop myself, I asked, "But let's just say—for the sake of argument—he was interested in me."

Emily grinned. "Oh, I like this game. Like, *what is the first thing you'd buy if you won the lottery?*"

I shook my head, but said, "Fine. Okay. Like that. Theoretically, let's say Luca—"

"*Luca?*" She giggled. "Oh, are you two on a first-name basis?"

Releasing a pained sigh, I debated whether or not to show her the emails and tell her about the kisses.

Kisses. As in plural of kiss.

Kisses that I couldn't keep myself from daydreaming about or reliving in the privacy of my bedroom. Those kisses.

"Just humor me." I endeavored to smile at my friend. "Let's say Professor Kroft was interested in me, what should I do?"

"Other than sit on his face?" She pursed her lips together, considering. "Maybe tie him up and take lots of pictures? Of course, pretend-Professor -Kroft would totally be into it."

"Emily."

"Anna."

"Be serious."

"I can't. This is a fantasy."

My sigh this time sounded more like a growl. "I need your help. I need you to listen and be serious for a minute."

Emily's grin faded and her eyes passed over me, dimmed with concern. "Fine. Let's be serious." Her words were halting.

"Remember the motorcycle guy? From last February?"

She nodded, the knit of her eyebrows betraying her continued confusion.

"That was Professor Kroft. You set me up with *Lucas Kraft*. And I accidentally emailed—"

She gasped, her hands flying to her mouth as her eyes bulged.

"—Luca Kroft. He met me at the restaurant, remember?"

Emily nodded wordlessly, still stunned.

"I had no idea when I signed up for his course. Then, the first day of the semester, we recognized each other and he asked me to stay after class."

I filled her in on the rest. I told her everything. The details erupting, a deluge of events colored by sporadic feelings and fears.

She was completely quiet except for additional gasps. Mostly, she just stared at me, dumbfounded.

"Professor Kroft," I paused, holding her gaze so she could see my uncertainty, then pulled the phone from my bag and showed her his latest email. "He sent me this, just after class."

I watched her read it, her eyes now at their maximum diameter.

"I don't know what to do," I confessed, turning off the phone and staring at the black screen. "I mean, he's the king of mixed messages, you know? And he's right, I am a lot younger than him. He's got to be—"

"Thirty-one," she blurted, her first words in over five minutes.

I nodded. "Right. So that makes him ten years older. And it's not just the age difference. Like he said, I'm immature. I'm goofy. I'm—I'm not his kind of nice." Repeating the words made my chest ache.

Emily finally blinked, as though waking from her trance of shock and awe. "This is incredible," she said to the room. "I mean, yeah. I can see why it happened, why he digs you."

"Really?" I asked, disliking, but resigned to, the disbelief in my voice. "He's sophisticated, a world scholar."

"He graduated from Oxford, post-grad at Princeton with a PhD in Russian Literature from the Slavic Department, top of his class."

Now it was my turn to gape at her.

She shrugged. "What? I looked him up after seeing his picture. I was curious."

Pushing aside the uncomfortable feelings inspired by her admission, I continued my earlier thought. "Right. So, he's this big deal, impressive professor. And I'm . . . ? What? An adequate waitress? A superb student? A juggernaut at jigsaw puzzles? Terrific at Trivia Tuesdays?"

"No. You *were* terrific at Trivia Tuesdays. Now you suck at Trivia Tuesdays because you're preoccupied. But, yes, I do understand why Professor Kroft digs you."

"Explain it to me." I grabbed her hand as I made the demand. "Because it doesn't make sense to me."

"First off, clearly he's attracted to what you look like. Let's just get that out of the way. He liked what he saw back in February, and he's probably not used to women disappearing on him."

"Okay. Fine. I accept this as fact, with the caveat that it has to be more than what I look like, because I'm nowhere near the best looking girl in the class."

Emily made a face. "See now, you underestimate yourself. You're a queen. A hot slice of co-ed cake. However," she held up her finger as though to stop me from interrupting her, "I will concede that I believe, as guys get older, it's less about 'the prettiest' and more about the intangible that makes a woman beautiful. It's about chemistry and shared passions. You've always been passionate about books. You read more —for fun—than anyone else I've met. Plus, your opinions are often radical, but never boring. You're creative and odd. And smart. And fun. And awesome. Maybe he's got the hots for your brain."

I kicked this theory around, deciding it was—at best —incomplete.

"He said I was immature."

"He called you, what was her name? Natasha?"

"That's right."

"And he implied he was Andrei? Then what draws Andrei to Natasha? Start there."

"Her cheerfulness," I recalled, thinking back on the book and trying to remember Andrei's first impressions. "But then later, her beauty and innocence. Andrei is a—" I struggled to describe the character and finally decided on, "He's world-weary. Jaded. He listens to her sing at one point and it inspired him to live his life more deeply. She's like a muse, for him to be a better man, to look at the world with new eyes. He's attracted to the idea of her, I think, more than the real her, especially at first. Or at least that's how Tolstoy wrote it."

Emily nodded, absorbing all this information. "Maybe that's why Professor Kroft runs hot and cold with you? He thinks he's attracted to the idea of you?"

"Maybe . . ."

Possibly.

"He's world-weary and jaded and there you are," she continued philosophically. "You don't throw yourself at him. In fact, you run in the other direction. Multiple times." She said this last part accusingly before adding more gently, "You're an enigma. You said he looked up your middle name?"

I nodded, confirming this.

"This is like a fairy tale." Emily sighed, leaning her elbow on the table and resting her chin in the palm of her hand.

I wrinkled my nose at her. "It's not like knowing my name gives him some power over me. I'm not Rumpel-stiltskin."

"Too bad he can't say it three times and your clothes fall off."

"Emily."

"Admit it. That would be awesome."

My cheeks heated, because I was thinking about it, and it

would be awesome. But I needed to get the conversation back on point.

"So what do I do?"

My friend stared at me for a long time, so long I didn't know if she was going to answer.

But then she said, "Forget him."

I released a breath and glanced at the ceiling of my apartment. "Be serious."

"I am. I'm being serious. I mean, I understand your hesitation. You like the guy, he's brilliant, engaging, charismatic, mysterious, and all that—more than just his handsome face—makes him sexy. He's definitely attracted to you, but he's also pushing you away just as much as he's pulling you in. So, forget him."

My mouth fell open, showcasing my shock, because that was not at all what I expected her to say.

"Truly?"

"Yes. Truly. He's tepid, not hot. If he can't see how fucking awesome you are, if he can't put himself on the line for you and go all in, pursue you like you deserve to be pursued, then—really—is he worth risking your heart? No. He's not. That makes him not *your* kind of nice."

My heart sank.

But she wasn't finished. "To clarify, your kind of nice doesn't play games. Sounds to me like he's a game player. He can't make up his mind, so he jerks you around. You don't need that shit. No amount of handsome is worth that kind of heartache."

"It's not his handsome that I'm attracted to. I mean, it *is* his handsome, but it's also—gah!"

"I know, I know. Like I said, it's everything—"

"Exactly."

"Except his cowardice. And that's a deal breaker."

My stomach and chest felt empty and I realized the sensation was disappointment. I was disappointed to an extreme degree.

"You're right," I conceded, willing away the heartache.

She gave me a sad, commiserating smile. "Sorry. As your best friend, I can give you no other advice."

I gazed at her, at my best friend and her best friend wisdom. "No. It's fine. It's what I needed to hear. Thank you for talking it through with me."

"No problem. And please do think of me should any other hot professors kiss your face off." Emily poked me with her celery stick as she stood. "I'm going to open that box of wine you've been saving. Tonight feels box o' wine worthy."

I still had Luca's champagne; it was in the back of my pantry. But I didn't want to drink it with Emily. The oddball in me had been saving it for him, for Luca.

"Fine. But we have to use my grandmother's china."

"Teacups?"

"Of course," I confirmed, reaching for my phone, "always teacups."

"Right-o." Emily turned and crossed my tiny apartment. She knew where I kept my grandmother's teacups because box o' wine nights always called for teacups.

Meanwhile, I opened my email, hitting reply to his, and tapped out a message to Luca. I decided that being blunt was the best course of action. At first, I typed everything I was thinking and feeling, a la,

Dear Luca,

As a preface to this message, I still firmly believe the source of Anna Karenina's sorrow and downfall was, fundamentally, lack of self-worth.

With that in mind, and in case you didn't know, I really like you. You're brilliant. You're an incredible teacher. I love talking to you, debating with you, listening to your thoughts. I love how passionate you are about matters of the soul and heart and mind.

Bonus, you're one of the few people in the world who looks good in leather pants *and* a bowtie (though maybe not at the same time . . . jury is still out).

But I also really like myself. Just as I am.

What I don't like is being kissed by someone who believes I'm not mature enough to, I don't know, date? (I hope you don't use the term 'Netflix and chill'). Even if that person's kiss is so blissfully transformative that the memory of him, of the touch of his lips, has infected every thought thereafter.

However, learning from Anna Karenina's abysmal example, I'm officially tapping out of whatever this thing is between us. I don't like games or game players. I might enjoy reading about wretchedness and epically tragic love stories, but I have no desire to live one.

As of now, I consider this resolved.

Wishing you the best with all your future endeavors,

Anna I. Harris

I reread the message, knowing it was good and honest. Yet I hesitated. It felt too . . .

Too . . .

Honest. Real. Naïve. Trusting. Vulnerable.

Unable to press the send button, I saved a draft and turned off my phone. I went to the bathroom, debating the length of the message, word choice, and nuances of sentence structure.

I was overthinking.

Leaving the bathroom, and frustrated with my lack of

action, I pulled up the email again, copied it and pasted it into a new message. Then I deleted all the parts that made me feel vulnerable, leaving me with,

Dear Luca,

I still firmly believe that the source of Anna Karenina's sorrow and downfall was, fundamentally, lack of self-worth.

Therefore, and learning from Anna Karenina's abysmal example, I'm officially tapping out of whatever this thing is between us. I consider this matter resolved.

Wishing you the best with all your future endeavors,
Anna I. Harris

Still honest. Still real. But without the messiness of putting myself out there. It felt safe. So I sent it.

"What should we drink to?" Emily appeared, holding two teacups full of wine.

I accepted my cup and clinked it against hers. "To being smart."

Emily gave me a small smile, saying nothing. I endeavored to return it as we both sipped our boxed wine and I congratulated myself on being smart.

And clearly having so much self-worth, that I never take any risks without a guarantee of success.

"Pass the box."

PART 15

** ANNA **

*W*e drank the entire box of wine.

And then I drank the vodka. Because I was still sad after the wine. Go figure.

Not surprisingly, it was a mistake.

A terrible, terrible mistake.

I had very strange dreams. Dreams of me rocking out to "I Am the Very Model of a Modern Major-General" from Gilbert and Sullivan's *Pirates of Penzance*. Dreams of me crying on the phone. Dreams of me destroying one of my framed jigsaw puzzles.

In the morning, instead of going for my walk, I knelt at the altar of the porcelain gods and prayed for the continued health and function of my liver. Then I went back to sleep only to be awoken by Emily setting a plate at my bedside with a loud clatter.

"Wake up, sunshine. I made you greasy food. And, you're welcome. I wrapped your hair in one of your silk scarves so you wouldn't wake up as the bride of Frankenstein."

I moaned into my pillow even as I touched the scarf at my forehead. This was the third time in my life I'd had a hangover; I could always count on regret and feeling like death, but at least this time my hair wouldn't be a catastrophe.

"Must you be so loud? Why do you hate me so much?"

"I'm whispering."

"You're a witch. Burn in a fire."

She cackled softly, but it sounded like a witch.

"Bacon, eggs, and toast. Get up and eat. Also," she called over her shoulder as she left my room, "your cell is on the pillow next to your head."

I moaned again, turning away from her offerings and dozing until my phone buzzed, sounding like a swarm of angry bees.

Someone was calling me, probably work asking me to fill in a shift.

Groaning, I blindly reached for the phone, my hand finding it instantly. I accepted the call, but then fumbled to bring it to my ear, finally answering with a pathetic, "Hello?"

"Anna?"

I paused, confused, because the voice on the other end didn't sound like Pedro from the restaurant.

"Who is this?" I croaked, lifting myself to an elbow and cracking an eye to check the caller ID; it read, *Prince Andrei Nikolayevich Bolkonsky.*

I scrunched my face, blinking several times at the nonsensical entry.

"You're awake," the man said, sighed, and then asked, "Are you sober yet?"

I'm not going to lie, I recognized Luca's voice almost instantly.

But I was also in denial, and denial is a blissful path on which to travel, the view is almost as nice as Ignorance Avenue.

And so, I decided the man on the phone couldn't possibly

be Luca because Luca didn't have my phone number. The man must've just been someone who sounded a lot like Luca.

Yeah. Yeah. That's the ticket.

I was allowed to inhabit this fuzzy limbo of obliviousness for precisely three seconds, until he said, "We need to talk about the emails."

And that was just the adrenaline shot needed to push me out of denial.

"What?" I shot up in my bed, immediately regretting this automatic response as a wave of nausea met a stab of pain and they became best friends. "Ugh, what emails?"

"The emails you sent me last night."

He did not sound happy.

"Don't— I mean how—" I gripped my head. I couldn't think, partially because I was hungover, but also partially because I was panicking. "I just sent one email."

Luca made a noise that sounded like a low growl, it made the hairs on the back of my neck prickle, but his voice was steady as he said, "I'll be in the office today. After you've read through your . . . messages, please come to my office on campus so we can discuss next steps."

"Next steps?" I croaked.

"Eat your breakfast," Emily's voice met my ears. "You're going to need it."

I lifted my eyes—with effort—to where my friend stood in the doorway, looking tired but not hungover. "What?"

"Eat your breakfast." She adjusted the strap of her bag on her shoulder, her mouth a flat line.

I could only gape at her dumbly, wondering if I was still asleep.

Maybe this is all a dream.

Before I'd recovered from her proclamation, she repeated, "You're going to need it," then turned and strolled out of my

room and out of my apartment, the front door closing softly—
yet still sounding like a cannon to my ears—as she left.

"See you soon, *malen'kaya lisa*," Andrei—I mean, Luca
—said, and I heard a motorcycle come to life on the other end
just before he clicked off.

Even though the line was dead, I held the phone to my ear
for a full minute, maybe longer. I was flabbergasted. Me,
frozen on my bed, unable to think or move—this continued
for some time.

And then I breathed. And I glanced around. And I tasted
the inside of my mouth.

"Shower. Toothbrush. Now!"

It was enough. Enough to get me out of bed and moving,
not thinking about the future, but thinking about the now. I
stripped, I showered, I brushed my teeth. I found a bottle of
ibuprofen and swallowed two pills with a glass of water.

Grabbing an outfit from the top of my folded laundry pile,
I quickly pulled on the navy cotton skirt and plain white T-
shirt, my heart lodged in my throat, my heart beating
sporadically.

"Calm down," I whispered, pressing a hand to my chest.
"Calm down."

A moment.

I just needed a moment to collect my thoughts.

Emails.

I turned to my bed and picked up my phone, trying to
remember any detail from last night that might explain what
happened. My fingers trembling, I navigated to my outbox
and flinched, counting six messages sent between 11:00 p.m.
and 2:30 a.m.

Sucking in a breath, I clicked on the first.

Luca, I've changed my mind. We should be friends with bene-fits. Here's my number for booty calls.

I groaned, dropping the phone to the comforter next to me, my heart lodged in my throat. "Shit, shit, shit, shit, shitty shitty shit shit!"

My face fell to my hands and I took several breaths meant to calm.

"I am such an asshole," I muttered to no one, "Anna the Asshole."

Once my heart slowed enough and my bravery reserves were somewhat replenished, I plucked the phone from the bed with grim resolve. To my surprise, he'd responded to my cheeky message,

Dear Anna, That's not what I want for us. Come to my office tomorrow. I must speak to you.
   -Luca

A surprised exhale escaped my lungs as I reread his note, my heart doing something new, fluttering in a way that was both painful and hopeful. But the compulsion to continue reading kept me from pausing to debate his meaning.

Dearest Andrei,
   Do you think Natasha would have been faithful to you if you'd given her a taste of physical intimacy? Do you blame yourself for her disloyalty? You should. Women need to be

touched. They crave it. I crave it. There are many ways to withhold oneself and all of them are painful.

-Your Natasha

Anna,

We should move this discussion off email. I'm calling you.

-L

Luca,

I'm not answering your call because I'm drunk and I might tell you the truth about how much I want to be with you and how much it hurts when you push me away. Better to email instead.

-Natasha

Luca,

Stop calling. I'm completely shitfaces and the slurring will be undignified.

Anna,

Are you safe? Is someone there with you?

Luca,

Yes. My friend Emily is here and she's not dtrunk she stopped after the wine bux but I found hte vodka

------

Anna,
What is Emily's phone number?

I frowned at his last message plus my response to it, where I sent him Emily's number, because a flash of something awful —a vague memory, a feeling of incensed righteousness— pressed forward in my consciousness.

Me.
Crying.
And yelling.
On the phone.
With Luca.

"Oh no." I shook my head, closing my eyes against the hazy recollection, my stomach sinking, then lurching. But before I gave in to my terror, I quickly texted Emily,

Me: What did I say to Luca last night?

    Emily: Go talk to him.

    Me: Tell me!!!

    Emily: Go talk to him.

    Me: Was I an asshole?

    Emily: Go talk to him.

    Me: You're a witch.

    Emily: Go talk to him. And eat your breakfast. You're going to need it.

"Traitor." I scowled at her texts even as another wave of nausea assaulted me. My stomach was empty and she was right, I needed to eat.

Grabbing the plate by the bed, I walked to the kitchen on unsteady feet and stuck the greasy breakfast in the microwave, heating it for twenty seconds as I scrolled through my emails to make sure I'd read all the messages.

I hadn't.

There was one more.

It was from Luca and the timestamp was before 11:00 p.m., before my drunk emails. It was in reply to the first message I'd sent last night, the one when I was sober and I'd informed him that I was *tapping out*.

The subject line was bolded, indicating that the message was still unread. Apparently, I hadn't seen it or opened it last night before my inappropriate drunkenness.

I tapped the email and read,

Dear Anna,

I've not been in this situation before, so you must forgive the imprecision of my actions. My instinct has been (and continues to be) to protect you, but I can no longer disregard my own wishes.

You mustn't attempt to drop the course again. However, my objectivity where you are concerned has been compromised. I approached the Department Chair regarding the situation last Monday and have since handed over your class portfolio.

This is what I wished to discuss with you tonight. Dr. McGovern has agreed to assume grading your assignments and he has appointed an impartial mediator for the remainder of the semester, an advocate for your interests.

For all intents and purposes, I am no longer your professor.

Thus, I do not consider this "thing" between us resolved. Far from it. I must see you. The place and time can be of your choosing, but let it be soon.

-Luca

* * *

I brought my backpack, but I left it in my car.

I don't know why I brought my backpack. I didn't need it, but going to campus without it felt strange.

The Slavic Department offices were vacant, much like they'd been that night when my feet and brain teamed up to confront Luca weeks ago. Paying homage to the déjà vu, I paused at the admin's desk and glanced down the long hall leading to his office.

This time his door was slightly ajar; a triangle of light spilled into the hallway, interrupted by shadowy movement from within.

He was in there.

And I was at a disadvantage.

Luca was the adult.

I was the impetuous child.

According to his email, he'd been going through appropriate channels, being responsible, taking measured steps to ensure we could explore whatever *this thing* was between us.

Meanwhile, I'd been moping. And drinking. And emailing him while intoxicated about booty calls, because I was too much of a coward to be completely honest while sober.

That ended now.

I'd changed into my business-casual attire—dark purple

skirt and white button down shirt, both ironed—pulled my hair into a bun as best I could, and opted for three inch heels over the Converse I usually wore.

I was prepared to be brave, to lay it all out there, to be reasonable and thoughtful and discuss.

Lifting my chin and straightening my spine, I marched down the hall to his office and knocked firmly on the door three times.

Swallowing my encroaching anxiety, I pushed it open just as he said, "Enter."

Heat spread like a wildfire through my body because Luca stood just inside, dressed in dark jeans and a gray T-shirt, his hair still tousled from his earlier motorcycle ride.

Must he be so handsome all the time? MUST HE??

Something flared behind his eyes when our gazes met, but otherwise his expression was blank. Or perhaps I didn't know how to read him.

"Luca," I nodded in greeting, infusing my tone with firm and detached resolve. "Is now a good time to meet?"

His gaze narrowed as it moved over my clothes, one of his eyebrows lifting just a fraction of an inch. He nodded slowly, crossing his arms, and I got the sense he was bracing himself—likely for whatever foolish, impulsive thing he thought I was about to say.

I stepped into his office, closed the door, and clasped my hands in front of me.

"First," I started, clearing my throat of the slight tremor. "I'd like to apologize for the emails I sent last night. It was . . . that was extremely inappropriate. I hope you will accept my apology."

Luca's gaze narrowed further and his jaw ticked, his lips pressing into an unhappy line. "Fine. Apology accepted."

"I appreciate that. And I assure you, it won't happen again." I nodded, giving him a tight, earnest smile.

Now, the hard part.

I gathered a breath for bravery, preparing to say what I'd rehearsed in the car on the way over.

But before I could, Luca's stare turned hard as he demanded, "Just say it."

I absorbed the anger behind his words and required a few seconds to steady myself, suppress the erratic and panicked beating of my heart. I knew—given the way I'd behaved—a distinct possibility existed that I'd lost my chance with him. It seemed that possibility had become a reality.

And that was okay.

Was it devastating? Yes.

Would I cry when I left? Yes.

Would I ever recover? I didn't know.

But I had to take responsibility for my actions, words, and decisions.

So be it.

Lifting my chin, I let my hands drop to my sides, preparing to wear my heart on my sleeve with abandon. "I'm ashamed I wasn't brave enough to tell you how I felt—how I feel—while sober."

Luca's eyebrows furrowed and his eyes skated over me again, cloudy with confusion. "Are you referring to the 'booty call' suggestion?"

"No." I released a self-deprecating huff and shook my head. "Not that one. I didn't read your response to my sober email until this morning, but that's not an excuse. I should have been braver. When you called me Natasha—"

My voice cracked. I was determined not to cry, so I took another breath and lowered my gaze to his neck; I couldn't look in his eyes if I was going to say this without bursting into tears like a nincompoop.

"When you called me Natasha, and told me to wait for my Pierre, you hurt my feelings. A lot. We don't—I mean—we haven't spoken to each other many times one-on-one, so perhaps I misunderstood your true intention, but it felt condescending, a bit like being patted on the head and being told I wasn't loyal, or trustworthy, or good enough—no, wait."

I held my hands up because Luca began moving forward.

"Let me finish." My gaze flickered to his and then away; I couldn't read his mood, but I knew I needed to complete my thoughts before I attempted to decipher his. "I'm realizing that I'm pretty terrible at nuanced situations, and that's something for me to work on. And since I'm bad at reading undercurrents and nuances, I need to ask—explicitly—for clarification. And I need to be explicit with my words. So this is me being explicit."

I was out of breath and the erratic beating of my heart had become a fierce gallop, but I was determined to do this right. I was determined to be brave. So I lifted my eyes to his, allowed our gazes to clash and tangle, and ignored the sound of blood rushing between my ears.

"I think you're amazing. Watching you with the class is inspiring. I love your passion for your work. I love how brilliant and thoughtful you are. And when you excluded me during class—"

"Anna—"

"When you ignored me, it was hurtful. And when you kissed me and told me to leave your office, that was hurtful. And when you sought me out at my work and took me to your apartment—"

"That wasn't my apartment."

"—and then compared me to a fictional character who

might be beautiful and spirited, but is too naïve to possess any real depth of feeling or sense of loyalty, that was also hurtful. I want to know you. And I'd like for you to know me. And if this is something that you want as well, then you're going to have to say or do something that leaves no room for doubt. But if you don't want to know me—"

I wasn't able to finish because Luca closed the distance between us with three large steps.

He grabbed me.

And he kissed me.

PART 16

＊ ANNA ＊

I gasped against his lips.

He captured the sound of surprise, crushing me to him, his fingers digging into my back and hip. Like the first time we'd kissed, I tasted hunger and annihilated restraint. But unlike before, the kiss wasn't frenzied. It was tender, gentle even, and at complete odds with how he held me.

Pressing his forehead to mine, he separated our mouths just long enough to say, "I never wanted to hurt you." He kissed me again, his tongue tasting my bottom lip. "I don't *want* to hurt you."

I grabbed fistfuls of his sweater and demanded between kisses, "Then tell me what you want."

"I want to know you," he said, holding my gaze and pressing me against the door with his imposing body.

A profound wave of relief crashed over me, then lifted me up, buoying my courage. "Anything else?" I grinned, clearly drunk with elation and relief.

He hesitated, his eyes growing hooded and lowering to my mouth. "Too many things, and I don't wish to frighten you." I shook my head, a denial on my lips, but he stopped my words with a quick kiss, saying, "You have been a subject of much fascination, for many months. Since February. When I watched you leave in those leather pants, withholding your middle name, and I knew you were running away."

"But I'm not—"

"And when you showed up in my classroom as someone else," his eyes moved to my hair and the attentions of his fingers followed; I felt him remove the pins from my bun, "someone more, but still the same, so mysterious, still running away."

I made a sound of frustration in the back of my throat, drawing his eyes back to mine. "I was not expecting you to be my professor. I think my freak-out was understandable and justifiable."

The side of his mouth curved upward. "And the fascination grew—with every test you turned in, every quiz, every paper relaying your thoughts. I read yours first. I searched for your name and read them immediately."

My hair fell from its incompetent twist and Luca pushed his fingers into the curls, bending to claim my lips with more maddeningly soft kisses.

"Every glance, every sight of you . . ."

"Luca," I breathed, my hands sliding to his sides; needing to feel him, I slipped my fingers under the hem of his sweater, and his skin jumped beneath my touch.

He hissed, sucking in a breath through his teeth, and his eyes grew dark. Luca dipped his head to my neck, kissing the sensitive skin just under my ear, whispering darkly, "I can't have you run away when I admit how much I've thought about this moment, how badly I want to touch you," kiss, bite, lick, "and taste you."

His large hands slid to my chest, lifting my shirt and bra

as he cupped my breasts, drawing his thumbs back and forth. I trembled, overheated with sensation and longing, and reached for his belt with shaking hands.

Blind desire.

That's what I felt.

Sightless and consuming.

My movements were clumsy, fueled by urgency and desperate *want*. Just as I'd unbuckled him, Luca seized my wrists with one hand and held them hostage above my head.

"I'm not interested in your regrets," his voice was rough and impatient. "If you—if we—"

"I won't be running away," I shook my head quickly and said between excited breaths, "I can't. I can barely walk in these shoes, have you seen the size of the heels?"

Amusement and appreciation flared behind his eyes, brightening them. "I adore this about you." Luca reached under my skirt and cupped me through my panties.

I gasped, then asked with forced lightness, "Oh? Really? You think you'll like this area of my body?"

"I do," he said, looking wolfish. "But I meant your words, how you speak. This is why you are Natasha to me."

As he said this, his lips lowered to the bared skin of my chest. Branding me, he bit and licked a cherishing path, causing me to buck instinctively, even as he moaned his appreciation.

The back of my head hit the door. Hard. I barely noticed, instead arching my back, offering more of myself.

But Luca lifted his head, tilting his chin backward to evade me as I chased his mouth, and pinned me with the hunger in his gaze. Saying nothing, he scrutinized me, as though greedy for my response. Each of my labored breaths flattened my exposed breasts to his chest.

"And this is why you're Andrei," I panted, allowing my

frustration to bleed into the words, "you can take me, you can have your Natasha. But you hesitate."

Luca's eyes narrowed as he trailed his hand upwards from where he cupped me, his palm pressing against my lower belly, and then slipped his hand into the waistband of my underwear, sliding his middle finger against my sensitive center.

A light tremor passed through him, his eyes flickering, half blinking, and he ground his teeth. I whimpered, my hips tilting, offering more of myself, even as my knees were in danger of buckling.

Maybe he sensed my weakness, or maybe he had his own agenda, but in the next moment he released my wrists, lifted my thighs, and picked me up. He turned, carrying me, and again conquered my mouth.

Luca placed my bottom on his desk, the slide of his tongue attentive, drawing my bottom lip between his teeth. His kisses turned rich and succulent, deliberate and relishing, as though he were consciously forcing himself to be mindful.

While distracting me with the sensuality of his lips and tongue, he divested me of my shirt and bra. His strong fingers hooked into my panties and he tugged, encouraging me to lift my backside, guiding them down my legs as he caressed light circles on the back of my knees and calves, sending jolts of deliciousness racing to my center.

But he made no move to remove my skirt, preferring instead to lift it, bunching the fabric around my waist.

Separating his mouth from mine, he trailed his gaze over my bare skin, his eyes now hooded, a dark indigo.

It was then, in that moment, as he devoured my body with his eyes, that I experienced the first hint of self-consciousness. And with self-consciousness came the sobriety of doubt.

Oh my God, oh my God, what the hell are we doing? We're in his office!

Abruptly, his eyes cut back to mine, as though he sensed the shift in me. Maybe he did sense it. Maybe my breathing gave me away, or the sudden fear causing my heart to stutter and then gallop.

I swallowed, barely resisting the urge to cover myself with my hands. "Luca?"

He shook his head, cupping my face and bringing my lips to his. Our mouths mated and again I melted, giving myself over to this new wave of yearning, heedless to anything that hovered beyond the periphery of *right now*.

Luca stepped between my thighs, widening them, and grabbed my backside. He brought me to the edge of the desk, my legs dangling.

I reached for his zipper, my knuckles pressing against the hard length of him, sending sensation ripe with anticipation singing through my veins.

But then he caught my wrists and he lifted his head.

And then he knelt on the floor.

And then his hands were on my knees.

And then he leaned forward.

And then he kissed me. And licked me. And moaned.

All the air left my lungs with a whoosh. I couldn't catch my breath. My hands on the desk found no purchase. Uncontainable sounds—of arousal and surprise—tumbled from my lips. I was so confused by what was happening. Elated and confused, and maybe a little scared.

My alarm only served to heighten the sensations caused by the skillfulness of his lips and teeth and tongue. Again his kisses grew rich and succulent.

Mindless words spilled out of me as I threaded my fingers

into his hair. Maybe I begged, perhaps I pleaded. It didn't matter. Nothing mattered except this feeling.

My thoughtless words of praise served only to encourage and invigorate him, and when he slipped two long fingers into me, I fell back on his desk, and pushed the base of my palms into my eyes. My mind and body splintered into a thousand perfect pieces of anguished bliss as I came with embarrassing swiftness.

I hadn't quite recovered when he removed his mouth from my body. I couldn't yet move in any meaningful way and I was still chasing my breath.

But I did peek at him from between my fingers.

I watched as he kissed the inside of my thigh, closed my legs, and placed another gentle kiss on my belly. He stood, his hands sliding from my knees to my hips. I saw him lick his lips, like he was tasting me there, and had to fight a shock of new arousal. His attention was on my skirt as he reached for the hem and covered me.

His eyes flickered over my form once, still hot and covetous, and then he turned away, giving me his back.

I removed my hands from my face, propping myself up on one elbow and covering my breasts with an arm. I watched his shoulders rise and fall. His head moved to the right and to the left, as though he was searching for something. Then he bent and retrieved the object.

Or rather, objects. He'd picked up my bra and shirt.

His gaze returned to my body and he set my clothes on the desk next to me. He paused, taking an expansive breath as his eyes again trailed over my form. As though just making up his mind about something, he bent, pushing my arms from my chest and lavishing my breasts with hungry, biting kisses.

"Luca—"

"I could do this all day." He murmured against my skin,

his fingertips sliding beneath the hem of my skirt and up my thigh once more.

Unable to speak, I grabbed handfuls of his shirt and tugged, wanting it off. Wanting his bare skin against mine.

And that's when he stopped, shifting his body such that his face was buried under my jaw. He gathered another expansive breath, held it, wrapping his arms around me, and exhaled my name against my neck, sending pinpricks of shivering sensation racing along my bare skin.

"Let's eat," he said, sounding regretful, pulling away.

"You just ate!" I blurted before I could catch the joke, digging my nails into the fabric covering his biceps to keep him in place.

A rumbly chuckle met my ears and I shivered again. I'd never heard him laugh before. He had an amazing laugh.

Lifting himself, he gazed down at me, his palms on either side of my head, braced against his desk.

"I want to know you, Anna," he whispered, placing his hand on my bare shoulder. He traced the soft skin of my collarbone and neck as his eyes moved between mine. "Let me know you."

PART 17

I wanted a shower.

As much as I'd like to be that girl who provides her guy an all-you-can-eat buffet downtown and doesn't bat an eyelash about hoisting up her panties and running errands afterward, I was not that girl.

Being fuzzy headed, floaty and loose after our sexcapades did not negate the need for a hose-down. Plus UTI's are no joke. If I wanted him to eat at my buffet again in the near future—and I did—then the place needed to be spic and span.

Now, I had to bring up the topic. Gracefully.

…

…

…

Try not to laugh yourself into apoplexy.

"What's wrong?"

I glanced at Luca, finding him glaring at me with suspicion. We were walking to my car. Or at least, I was walking to my car. He was walking next to me as we were about to go grab a bite to eat and presumably get to know each other better.

"Nothing." My voice was too high.

He released a frustrated breath, gritting his teeth. I could see he didn't believe me and was likely jumping to the wrong conclusions.

"I'm really, really good." I placed a hand on his arm, stopping him so he'd look at me.

"This is why Andrei didn't touch Natasha," he murmured bitterly, then lifted his hardened voice to address me. "It was too soon and you're regretting it."

"It wasn't too soon." I flexed my fingers on his arm.

"Then tell me what's wrong."

"Nothing is wrong."

"Sure. Okay." He gave his head a subtle shake, the dimming of his eyes communicating volumes more than his words.

"Dammit, Luca." I grabbed his other arm, frowning at him severely before lifting to my toes and whispering harshly in his ear, "I need a shower, okay? Are you satisfied? I was trying to figure out how to bring it up. And I didn't want to be unsophisticated about it and say, *I need a shower because it's good hygiene after oral stimulation of the vulva and clitoris.*"

Luca's body tensed, a short sound of surprise—maybe also humor—erupted from his chest, and his broad palms pressed against my lower back, holding me in place.

"So you see," I continued, "rather than discuss or make comparisons between the microbe content in human saliva versus—I don't know—a dog, I thought I'd try to gracefully suggest we go back to my place to change." I leaned away to catch his eyes, but not very far because he continued to press my body against his.

The side of his mouth was curved in an appreciative but small smile and his eyes were once again bright, almost merry. All semblance of his earlier frustration now absent.

"Don't change," he said, his gaze drifting over my forehead, nose, and lips.

"But I need to change." I grimaced. "Like I said, I need a shower."

"That's not what I meant. We'll go to my place, I'll order in, you take a shower. Change your clothes, fine. But," his eyes met mine and they looked distinctly hazy, "don't change yourself. Never try to be other than you are. You are perfection, just as you are."

My eyes widened and my grimace morphed into something else, something plagued with worry. "Perfection is a lot of pressure. I can't live up to perfect. Not even in mathematical terms."

"Mathematical terms?"

"Like a perfect number. When the sum of its divisors—except the number itself—equals the given number."

His smile grew, though his brow furrowed. "You lost me. Math has never been a strength."

"Ah!" I shifted out of his grip, turning towards my car. "Are you telling me you can't math?"

Luca caught my hand before I moved too far away, entwining our fingers together as we walked side-by-side. The gesture made my breath quicken, my step falter, and my heart do wonderful, achy things. Perhaps even more wonderful than when his mouth had devoured my body.

"No. I can't math."

"Don't worry, gorgeous. You still have your looks. And you're well spoken." I tried to maintain a serious expression but lost it when I spied his narrowed glare.

He laughed at me and I laughed with abandon. Though my laughter was tinged with hysteria because, and I know this was odd, I'd never held hands with another person before, not even past boyfriends. It just never came up. Funny how such a simple, affectionate display could twist me into such devastating and beautiful knots.

I sensed Luca study me again. "Still thinking about the shower?" he guessed, likely picking up on my odd change in breathing.

I shook my head, deciding to answer with complete honesty this time. "No. I was just thinking how nice your hand feels." I swallowed, forcing myself to meet his gaze, finishing softly, "How nice it feels in my hand."

An immediate grin split his features, which he quickly attempted to subdue, clearing his throat. "See? Was that so hard?"

"What?" I asked breathlessly, still feeling winded by the sensation of his masculine fingers sliding against mine.

Luca wrapped his arm around me and kissed my temple. He bent, nuzzling and whispering against my ear, "Being you."

* * *

I drove my rust bucket, following Luca on his motorcycle and enjoying every moment of the drive, especially when we hit two red lights and he was forced to straddle his bike.

You straddle that bike, professor. You straddle it so hard.

Heh. Good times.

My ex-professor lived in a small two-bedroom house near the university, in one of the oldest areas of the city. The sidewalks were lined with giant, sloping trees and several of the houses had stained glass windows facing the streets.

He explained, as we walked to his door, that his house used to be an outbuilding for the much larger, grander mansion on the next street over. But that the property had been divided over time so that more houses could be built and a neighborhood could develop.

Despite being small, his home was exceptionally and tastefully decorated. The interior screamed sophisticated man-cave. You know, of the sipping cognac, classical music, and a smoking jacket variety. Basically, the room used by the host for *Masterpiece Theatre* (not theater, *theatre*).

Worn leather sofa, ancient looking Kashmir rug, dark wood trim against white walls, antique furniture, and inset bookcases added to the overall ambiance of cozy elegance. Additionally, and oddly, the front room had a fireplace the size of a walk-in closet.

"Nice fireplace," I said automatically, unable to miss the massive, redbrick chimney, the hearth as tall as I was. It spanned nearly the entire wall. In fact, several of me could fit inside it.

"Yeah, it's unusual for a fireplace in America, I know. My sister—who's the expert on these kinds of things—says this building might have been the servant's kitchen. That fireplace was used to cook meals for hundreds of people. There's another fireplace in the back of the house, much smaller."

I lifted an eyebrow at a bookcase to the left but still within the hearth, my gaze also snagging on the wall to my left which was inlayed with shelves from floor to ceiling, and each of those shelves was laden with hundreds of books.

"That's a lot of books." I tried not to salivate, though my fingers itched to touch them, pet their spines and smell their pages.

"It is," he agreed evenly.

I didn't have to look at Luca to know he was smile-smirking.

"I love you," I murmured distractedly.

"Pardon?"

"Shh," I waved Luca off without looking at him, "I was talking to the books. Maybe you could give us a moment?"

A rumbly chuckle met my ears, followed by a sigh. I heard his footsteps approach just before his hands slid around my middle, and he placed a lingering kiss on the sensitive skin beneath my ear.

His hot breath spilled over my neck as he said, "Sure. I'll go get you a towel for your shower. Try not to molest my books while I'm gone."

"I make no promises."

I knew he was still grinning as he left and that made me grin, even enraptured as I was by the ancient tomes before me.

Apparently, Luca owned every version of every piece of notable Russian literature ever written. In multiple languages. Beautiful leather spines in burgundy, navy, and forest green called to me, the gold leaf lettering glittering in the late afternoon sun filtering through stained glass windows.

To me the room had the picturesque aura of what I imagined an old church or a monastery would possess, the quiet sacredness, the tranquil purity. How I would love to spend evenings curled up on the inviting sofa by a small fire, tucked under one his wool blankets, reading Chekhov or Pushkin. Or maybe Luca would read them to me in the original Russian.

No.

That was a bad idea.

It was very likely I would trade sexual favors for Luca reading to me in Russian. And I'd enjoy every minute of it.

"What are you in the mood for?" Luca's voice reached me from wherever he was, presumably looking for a towel.

"Poetry and fellatio," I said under my breath, tracing my finger over the spine of Pushkin's collected poetry.

"I didn't catch that." Luca appeared in the doorway to my left.

I released a pained sigh, turning to him. "I really like your books."

"Thank you." He gave me a secretive smile, which widened the longer he studied my expression, which was likely wistful. "Let me show you where the shower is."

He turned, motioning for me to follow, which I did, somehow not surprised to find he'd placed—or someone had placed—a bookshelf along the wall and close to the ceiling. And there again, in the bathroom, I was met with more books.

"This is the guest bathroom," he explained, shoving his hands in his pockets as he lingered outside the door.

"I see." I took a moment to read several of the spines, all contemporary fiction, before turning to face him. "Thank you. I'll try to be quick."

"Take your time." He nodded tightly, his eyes moving quickly down and then up my body as he swallowed. "Do you have a taste for anything?"

I considered him and his question, a traitorous *your abdominal muscles, biceps, and thighs* springing to my mind, but I knew he meant actual food. Not man food.

Not. Man. Food.

"I'll eat anything," I said on a rush, feeling a slow, creeping blush spreading upwards to claim my cheeks. Gripping the edge of the door, I pushed it forward, forcing him to take a step back. "And I promise I'll be fast."

Behind the closed door, I released a heavy sigh and stripped. I was grateful to be alone so I could collect my thoughts and hormones, grateful for the shower for obvious reasons, also grateful I'd held myself in check and hadn't (yet) thrown myself at Luca and his big . . . library.

* * *

"You are completely insane."

"Because I make an argument for counter-enlighten-ment?" Luca's elbow rested on the back of the sofa and he was biting the tip of his thumb, his wolfish stare twinkling at me, as though he was enjoying my display of temper.

"Because you misrepresent nihilism as counter-enlighten-ment and are only doing so because you are attempting to irri-tate me."

Luca grinned, his eyes growing hooded as they dropped to my lips. "Are you irritated?"

"You know I'm irritated." I arched my eyebrows in chal-lenge. We'd finished dinner hours ago, and had been sitting on the sofa, facing each other on opposite sides. My feet were tucked under my body as I sipped on my second glass of wine.

And let me tell you, this was really good wine. *Really* good.

His grin spread, as though irritating me had been his heart's desire. "What can I do to make it up to you?"

"Admit you're wrong." I glowered at him. Or at least I tried to glower at him. It was hard to glower at Luca.

His look was equal parts teasing and skeptical. "That's not what you want."

"Oh? Really?"

"Yes. I know you better than you think. Remember, I've read all your papers."

"And I've attended most of your lectures. And seen you in leather pants."

He ignored that, continuing as though I hadn't spoken. "You want me to tell you that your proclivity and bias towards romanticism makes you blind to the—"

I scoffed loudly, inelegantly, setting my drink on the table behind the sofa and squeezed my eyes shut, "I'm not listening to this. You're just being contrary to be contrary. If you continue in this manner I shall sing *Pirates of Penzance* very loudly until you cease and desist."

Luca's deep laughter met my ears before I'd finished my threat. He reached for me, tugging me forward and placing a kiss on my mouth, like he couldn't help himself, catching my bottom lip with a gentle bite. A thrill raced through me, sparks of happiness tightened my lungs, desire pooling low in my abdomen. But instead of pulling me closer, he set me away.

I peeked at him, opening only one eye, and found him grinning at me. "You seem to be smiling a lot." I couldn't keep the discontent from my tone.

"You make me smile." Luca was biting the tip of his thumb again, his happy expression melting away any disappointment I felt about the laconic nature of our kiss.

Opening my other eye, I squinted at him. "Tell me something."

"Ask me anything."

"That night, during the first week of the semester, when you stopped by my restaurant. Who were you with? Those people at your table?"

Some of the mirth and good vibes drained from Luca's features. "That was my family."

"Are you Russian? I mean, are you from Russia?"

He nodded, though he said, "Yes. And no."

"Which is it?"

"I mean, I am Russian. My mother was born in Switzerland, but she is Russian. My father was born in Ukraine, but he is also Russian. Both sets of my grandparents left Russia in the early days of the USSR. I was born in Switzerland."

"Oh." I sat straighter in my seat, trying to assemble the puzzle pieces while I volunteered, "I was born in Springfield."

"Illinois?"

"No. Springfield, Transylvania."

He flashed an amused smile, tilting his head just slightly.

I was pleased to see his good humor return. "So, Switzerland?"

"Yes."

"And? Did you grow up there?"

"Not all the time."

"You're being vague, Luca." I lifted my eyebrows at him and pointed at his face. "Stop being vague."

He expelled an audible breath, glancing over my shoulder. "Fine. My grandparents own—or they *owned*—a diamond mine in Russia, sold it to the government and invested the money in global markets. They've done well for themselves, investing the money."

"Why don't you sound happy about that?"

He didn't look happy about it either, much of the light had left his eyes.

Luca shrugged, his gaze moving up and to the left. "I see the world clearly, now that I am older, and I'm disappointed by the country of my grandfathers. Russia used to be great, a nation of philosophers, brilliant thinkers, artists, and scientists. Not anymore. It hasn't been great for a long time, not since Stalin purged the thinking class. Contrary to popular belief, he didn't murder the bourgeoisie, he murdered anyone with *talent*. Do you know what that does to a society? I find it's difficult to be proud of my heritage, of a culture I now consider mediocre at best, monstrous at worst. Russia is irrevocably crippled, stained by its totalitarianism—to which it still subscribes, like sheep—and rivers flow, the sky weeps with the blood of what once made it great."

Despite the stark nature of the topic, I found myself falling under the spell of his poetic prose. Unthinkingly, I said on a sigh, "You should write a book."

His eyes cut to mine and bemusement lingered behind them. "Actually, I am."

"You are?" I bounced in my seat—just once—excited by the prospect of Luca writing a book.

"Yes. And it's horribly depressing. It's about a professor in Stalin's Russia—USSR—and everyone dies."

I'm a sick, sick individual, because the description made me smile with enthusiasm. "That sounds awesome. Please tell me there is doomed love."

He chuckled. "Yes. There is a tragic love story. I doubt anyone will read it. But it's a story I feel is important in order for the West to understand modern Russia."

"Can I read it?" I blurted, before I could think better of the request.

He didn't give me even a second to regret the overly familiar and downright invasive entreaty, nodding once and saying, "You may. If you wish."

"I do wish. I wish very, very hard."

"You might be the only one who does read it." He regarded me with what I recognized as open affection, causing my heart to do another of those achy, tight, hot flutters. "Literature and philosophy, questions of the soul and the purpose of being, these are dying pastimes."

"What do you mean?"

"I mean there's no money to be made in explaining the motivations of dead artists, in teaching people to think critically, carefully, to know themselves. Departments like medicine and engineering—the *essentials,* as they're called

—bring most of the cash flow into the university, subsidizing departments like mine. If we can't write a book, secure grants or endowments—which are very rare—then we're moved to adjunct positions, with no benefits or security."

"Have you? Applied for grants?"

"Yes. Tons. I've received some—smaller ones, but still enough to cover my publishing and writing time—but not nearly enough to justify my existence."

I frowned. "Are you, I mean, are they moving you to an adjunct—"

"No." He shook his head, an unmistakable bitterness flavoring his words as his gaze moved to his glass of vodka. "My family is quite wealthy and have donated an endowed chair in my name to the university. My position is very secure."

Studying him, the undercurrent of frustration behind his words and the line of his mouth, I pressed, "And that bothers you?"

His eyes cut to mine. "Of course it bothers me. I put myself through school—partially with academic scholarships, yes—but also by working the whole time, paying my own way. I didn't discover that my job offer was contingent on the endowed chair until months *after* I'd accepted the position."

"Why didn't you leave? Go elsewhere?"

"Because the endowment doesn't just pay my salary. It saved half the tenured positions in the department," he admitted quietly, looking solemn, and maybe a little sad.

"Hmm." I studied Luca, recognizing the fierce disappointment in himself for what is was. He'd clearly wanted to make his own way in the world, separate from his past, but—unbeknownst to him—his family had taken that decision away.

However. "But hasn't that always been the way of art?"

"What do you mean?" Luca regarded me over the rim of his glass, lifting an eyebrow in question.

"Haven't industrialists paid the salary of artists for centuries? And before that, rich merchants sponsored them? And before that, the masses did so through taxes and tithes paid to governments and churches? Hasn't each global society subsidized art and artists? Been patrons for philosophers, authors, and poets? Isn't that just the way of the world?"

Luca frowned thoughtfully, still looking unhappy.

I gave him a small smile. "I'll graduate with a degree in electrical engineering this coming spring, and after that I want to get a master's degree and a professional engineer license. Do you know why?"

"Because you're good at the math," he deadpanned.

"No." I laughed, shaking my head at his dour expression. "That's not why. Though I am *good at the math.* But other than that, other than enjoying math and science and being pretty darn good at them both, I want to make money. I want to have a job where I can support myself and my reading habit."

A wrinkle of curiosity and confusion appeared between his eyebrows. "You may enjoy math and science, but you *love* literature. I see it, I know you do."

"You're right. I love to read, but I'm not a writer. I love philosophy, but I'm not a philosopher. I love art, but I can't paint, I can't draw or sculpt. I love movies and the theater, but I'm a terrible actor. Therefore, I'm a patron," I finished proudly.

As I spoke his expression cleared, his eyes growing sober with understanding and—if I was reading him correctly— with respect.

I continued, "Don't worry, the world will always need art,

and artists, and literature. Just like it will always need industry and medicine. One is not more or less important than the other, at least I don't think so. Why do we have art? To make life beautiful, to understand each other. And why do we have science? To make life easier."

"And you don't think you're a philosopher?" Luca's eyes moved between mine, a quiet kind of appreciation making his features even more handsome.

That made me grin. "I'm not. But sometimes I pretend to be when I'm debating with my—" I cut myself off, catching the word *boyfriend* before it left my mouth, and swallowed instead.

Luca's gaze flared, and grew intent, watchful. "With your what?" he asked slowly, setting his drink to one side but never taking his eyes from mine.

"With my lover," I said with faux-haughtiness.

His eyes flared again. "Not your boyfriend?"

"No. You're not a boy."

"False."

"You know what I mean."

"Fine," he leaned forward, his gaze dropping to my lips, "call me *lyubov moya*."

My lashes fluttered at his use of Russian, other parts of me fluttered as well. "Um, what-what does that mean?"

"And I'll call you *malen'kaya lisa.*"

"Oh my," I breathed, attempting to swallow. "That better mean badass."

"It means little fox." His voice dropped, his hand sliding from my knee, and up my skirt. "Which I believe is very apt."

"Okay," I agreed, because . . . sexy. *Like a fox.*

"*Malen'kaya lisa*," he whispered, bending to my neck before whispering, "*Lyubov moya.*"

"Yes." I gripped his shoulders for balance, figuratively and literally.

I was sitting on the couch, theoretically in no danger of falling off said couch, but I was also dizzy.

So. Dizzy.

Things between us were moving quickly and my heart was full speed ahead. I didn't know if I could put on the brakes, even if I wanted to. But I didn't want to. What I wanted was more—of him, of this, of us—and I wanted it all now.

Was he too old for me? Was I too young for him? Would the differences in our ages and circumstances, life experience, and bank accounts ultimately prove too much to overcome?

Maybe more importantly, was he my kind of nice?

Perhaps.

Perhaps not.

But, ultimately, what did it matter?

"Anna, spend the night." His fingers inched higher, dancing lightly over my skin, then retreating. "Spend the night with me. We'll take things slow, but," he placed a kiss on my jaw, "stay with me." Another on my chin. "Wear my shirt, let me watch the morning caress your hair and flawless skin, read the paper with me in bed, let me—"

"Yes to everything after the word Anna," I blurted, eliciting a delicious, rumbly chuckle, which ended abruptly as I palmed the front of his pants and stroked.

Damn, he felt good.

If Russian literature and tragic novels had taught me one thing it was this: disappointment and heartache might be around the next corner. But adventure, love, joy, and happiness—the living of a rich, meaningful life—was now.

And let us not forget about the ever present possibility of a nearby, but yet undetected blood illness.

Yes.

Better to make out with my hot, brainy ex-professor now, just in case a blood illness is lurking around the corner!

"I think you are going to be the death of me, Andrei." I captured one of his hands, moving his fingers under my shirt, encouraging him to palm my breast, and moaning when he did so.

"No." His gaze grew impossibly dark, his eyes now a deep indigo, holding mine captive.

"No?" I cupped his jaw, placing a fervent kiss on the corner of his mouth, wanting his lips on mine.

"Not death, Natasha." His words held a dangerous edge, as though the reins of his restraint were near breaking, yet he managed to whisper harshly, "I suspect we will be the *life* of each other," just before he claimed me with a soul deep, heart recalibrating kiss.

And I knew, my course had been irrevocably altered. My future reshaped.

Nothing in my life would ever be the same.

EPILOGUE (IN TWO PARTS)

What is my life?

I awoke, acutely aware of the man curled behind me, his arms wrapped around my waist after another night of sleeping together.

To be precise, we were on night number four of sleeping together. And on each of these four nights we'd cuddled—fully clothed—but mostly slept.

That's not so say we'd been "together" for just four days. No. We were now entering our second month of being "together," and yet had spent just four nights—including our first night—sharing a bed. Where we'd slept.

Just slept.

Like that first night.

When Luca Kroft said he planned to take things slow, I discovered what he really meant was putting a big old pin in hanky-panky and making up for all the conversations we'd missed while he was pretending I didn't exist.

Luca and I now saw each other all the time, and *that* was glorious. We ate at least two meals together each day. We discussed the logical fallacies of nihilism and debated its pragmatic uselessness; we both agreed: pragmatically speaking, nihilism was useless.

We talked about everything, impassioned conversations covering a wide range of topics, from the changing nature and utility of beauty to the evolution of primetime television (from must- see to Netflix binge-watching).

We'd even discussed the fact that I was on birth control, and that we were both clean, and how careful we'd both been in the past with sexual partners.

And yet, every night, after a handful of heated kisses, he'd set me away, leave me hot and bothered. And aching.

So much aching.

It was the kind of ache that would make Dostoyevsky proud.

But rarely, like last night, when we'd talk and lose track of time, and the hour grew ridiculously late, Luca would be too tired to drive home. He would stay over.

And sleep.

Just. Sleep.

Oh, Andrei. You rascal, you. Giving Natasha a taste of the forbidden apple and then withholding all your tasty, tasty fruit.

To put it another way, Luca was a fruit hoarder.

I'd considered bringing up his habit of kissing me senseless and then abandoning me to my wretched unrequited passion. I'd thought about it *a lot.* But ultimately, I didn't.

Because the truth was, I enjoyed his fruit hoarding. I loved the anticipation, each kiss an inferno, every time we said goodbye I burned and pined until we met again.

I loved it.

Maybe I'm a masochist? Hmm . . . could be.

But do I care? Hmm . . . no, I don't.

So instead of focusing on what we hadn't yet shared, I focused on enjoying his company and squeezing every ounce of awesome out of our moments together, memorizing the way he laughed at my jokes. Or how he'd bite his thumb and gaze at me like I was wonderful when I was in the middle of a particularly heartfelt speech. Or his habit of holding my hand and kissing my knuckles, each one in turn, while his stare held mine, transfixed. Or how he'd sigh—sometimes dejected, sometimes frustrated, rarely with amusement—when reading and grading the papers of my classmates. Or how he brought me a single lily each time he picked me up after my evening shift at the museum restaurant. Or how he left me sweet notes on my kitchen counter, notes I wouldn't discover until after he'd already left.

Or how he appeared to be just as frustrated and greedy for more sexy times as I was, but held himself in check with impressive restraint. I loved watching his control thin and shred, how each time he pulled away at the end of the night he'd grow quiet and surly, and pace, and then leave, as though a quiet thunderstorm had taken up permanent residence within him.

In this regard, he was so deliciously unusual.

As Luca and I lived in a modern world, very little (logistically) kept us from sealing the deal, what with the advent of birth control and safe sex practices. Yet, for whatever reason, we didn't.

He wanted to wait. He'd never said as much out loud, but his actions made his intentions obvious.

And it was a beautiful, torturous thing.

He was so great, and being with him was easy and *so great,* and I absolutely loved every second of the time we shared. So why would I complicate—i.e. ruin—things by complaining about the turtle pace of our physical intimacy?

I wouldn't and I didn't.

I ached, and it hurt so good, and *this* was my life, and I loved it so much.

So I squeezed his arm where it wrapped around me. I closed my eyes. I took a deep breath, enjoying the twistings and achings and flutterings. I wanted to remember these sensations for the rest of my life, however long they might last.

"Anna?"

I stiffened, feeling a little caught by his wakefulness. I'd been having a private moment of reflection and wasn't quite ready to leave my languid ponderings.

Although, as good feelings about Luca were the source of my languid ponderings, I soon got over the interruption. Especially since Luca's voice reminded me of charcoal first thing in the morning, smoky and deep, dark and uninhibited.

I'd learned over the last two months that he was most susceptible to seduction in the morning. I assumed this was why we'd only spent the night together four times. His hands seemed to roam freer and were more likely to breach clothing, to caress bare skin—as he was doing now.

"How long have you been awake?" His hand smoothed from my waist to my hip, and on the return pass his fingers slipped beneath my night shirt, trailing along my stomach to my ribs.

"Not long." The words were breathless and I held perfectly still, not wanting to move and draw attention to his instinctive ministrations. I suspected he didn't realize what he was doing, or he hadn't quite cleared his brain of the dream-fog yet.

When he did, when he realized his hand was under my

shirt, he would draw away and sit on the edge of the bed, taking a few deep breaths before making some excuse to leave the room—or so that had been the pattern thus far.

For now, I held my breath as the backs of his fingers brushed lightly against the underside of my breast, and I couldn't stop the automatic urge to arch my back, and press my bottom against him. But I did successfully bite back the moan that threatened to tumble from my lips when I found his body ready—so ready—for mine.

Luca's breathing grew ragged and he pressed forward, rocking against my backside as his hand became bolder, sliding to fully cup my breast, massage it, sending a shot of pleasure and pain low to my abdomen, and lower still.

"Anna," he breathed against my neck, biting my shoulder like he wanted to consume me. "We should stop."

Sensing his gathering control and intention to draw away, I grabbed his hand and pressed it more firmly against me, forcing it lower, down my stomach, beneath my underwear, to the thrilling ache between my legs. All the while meeting the indolent rhythm of his hips with my bottom.

"Touch me, Luca," I moaned.

What is this life?

Was this me? Had I become *this* kind of nice? This bold, demanding, aching kind of nice? I hoped so. I felt like this kind of nice would probably get me laid more often, and with more intense satisfaction.

Luca made a sound like a growl, deep in the back of his throat and rumbling in his chest, but didn't pull away. Instead, he indulged my request, and in doing so, he pushed me to the precipice, where longing and mindlessness, and pain and pleasure dance on the edge of oblivion.

Oh God, I was so close. *So close.* But then he moved away after a few strokes, shifting to one side and placing me on my back until I lay next to him while he lounged on his side. His hand now stroked me lightly over my underwear.

Ugh.

Torture.

PURE TORTURE.

Sweet, succulent, delicious torture.

But it didn't matter. I was so hyped, I was likely going to come anyway. I felt the first tell-tale signs as a surge of heat rushed over my neck to my cheeks, and my hips moved to music I couldn't hear.

He bent to my ear, hot breath and whispered words falling over the sensitive skin of my neck, "You infect me, body and soul, with primitive thoughts of claiming and conquering. I do not know who I am when I touch you. I am no longer civilized, I am blood and heat and lust. I barely recognize myself."

Paying no attention to any potential nuance within his meaning, I focused solely on the key words: claiming, blood, heat, and lust.

All good words. I liked those words.

But then he moved as though to withdraw fully. Unthinkingly, I grabbed his wrist and opened my eyes to meet his.

He glared at me. Actually, we glared at each other. An unspoken challenge hung heavy between us. Or that heaviness might have been his erection against my hip.

Seconds ticked by, maybe a full minute, and I sighed the intense sigh of sexual frustration, covering my face with my hands. I felt him hesitate beside me, his weight still on the bed, as I concocted a plan to finish up business while he took a shower, or maybe after he left, or whatever.

"Anna."

"What?" I pulled my hands away and looked at him.

His jaw ticked, his eyes—hot and covetous—moved over

my face, and his lips were parted as though he was about to speak; whatever it was, it seemed to be something of great importance.

Finally, he said, "I'll make breakfast."

I nodded, only half paying attention, because my body was still humming. In fact, I was trailing my fingers back and forth over my exposed stomach, enjoying the feel of my soft skin.

His attention snagged on the movement of my hand, his jaw ticking once more as he seemed to grind his teeth.

"Anna. . ." This time my name was a tight whisper, and sounded suspiciously like a plea.

I didn't know what he wanted, what he was asking me for. But I knew what I wanted. So I hooked my thumbs in my shorts and underwear; that movement also drew his attention. Slowly, I pushed the clothes down my legs and studied his shocked expression with satisfaction as his chest expanded with a bracing breath.

And still, he didn't move. His hand now rested on my upper thigh, his palm hot against my leg, and he watched—a scarcely subdued thunderstorm—as I hitched my shirt upward, revealing my breasts, then trailed my hand along my stomach, over the ache in my abdomen, and spread my legs.

He flinched when my fingers made contact with my body, and his breath returned, labored as he watched me touch myself.

What am I doing? What is this life?

Goosebumps erupted over the whole of my exposed skin and I felt every nerve ending spark and fire where his eyes moved, devoured, claimed and conquered in a way he wouldn't yet allow himself to do.

As though unable to help himself, he bent and sucked my breast into his hot, wet mouth, his fingertips trailing a tickling, restless path along my inner thigh, to my knee, as his tongue tangled with and lapped at my nipple.

I felt something stir within him and he shifted, a break or a decision to act.

But it was too late.

I arched, throwing my head back, caring only about the high of sensation. And I soared.

* * *

"But the underlying passion behind Eugene's discontent is what drives Tatyana at the first. She knows as soon as she sees him."

Luca shook his head, glaring at me. The covetous heat from earlier this morning hadn't quite left his eyes; rather, it simmered, and had begun turning the clear blue of his irises a rather particular shade of gray. I decided the color should be called "'the gray of my discontent.".'

"No. You are missing the entire point." Luca stood, grabbing his plate and mine and stomping to the sink. "Eugene is passionless. He's a miserable person. He was miserable without Tatyana. He would have been miserable with her, because his existence has no purpose."

"Tatyana didn't think so." I watched his profile as he did the dishes.

"It's an allegory of the time," he shook his head, clearly frustrated, "of the privileged class and their ennui, while the proletariat suffers. There is no cure for ennui, just like there is no cure for starvation, save death."

"That's not true." I reached for my coffee cup and stood, crossing to where he was finishing up the last plate. "The cure for starvation is nourishment. Don't you think it's possible that Tatyana could have been the nourishment that he needed? You say he had no purpose, but couldn't Tatyana—and her passion and love for him—couldn't that have become his purpose?"

"But how healthy is that?" He gave me a face, turning off the water and drying his hands., "How healthy is making another person your purpose?"

"Who cares?" I said louder than necessary, grinning at him. "Who cares how healthy it is? When you're talking about the reality of starvation and death, what's a little codependence?"

Luca stared at me for several seconds, and then—abruptly—he laughed, heartily, shaking his head. "You are completely mad."

I grinned, an acute sense of triumph making me stand taller as the discontented gray of his eyes had warmed, now bluer, less cloudy.

My heart skipped as I continued. "Seriously, who cares? Something I think we forget, living in the time we do, is that generations before us didn't have the luxury of healthy relationships. They had survival."

"And passion," he added, his eyes dropping to my lips as his smile waned.

"And high infant mortality. And cholera."

"And love."

Whoa.

An involuntary flurry of something *fantastic* hit me like an electric shock, originating in my chest and radiating outward.

But then I noticed the smile had leached from his face, leaving his jaw set in a mournful line and his eyes that melancholy gray once more. "But only those who were free to do so."

"Free to do what?" I tilted my head to the side as I took a

step closer such that mere inches separated us, accidentally bumping his leg with mine.

"Free to love." Luca shook his head as though frustrated.

I bumped his leg again, this time on purpose, forcing his eyes back to mine. "I guess it's a good thing we live now."

His smile grim, he wrapped his hand around the back of my head and brought my forehead to his lips for a kiss. His arms slid around me and I set my coffee cup on the counter so I could return his embrace.

"I'll see you for dinner?"

I nodded against his chest, giving him a squeeze. "I'll meet you after my last class." We were in the second week of the fall semester and were already falling into a routine. After my classes, I'd go to his office and study while he worked. Then we'd have dinner together, usually at my place as I didn't like driving home past midnight, which was when we usually said our goodbyes.

"Do you work tomorrow?" He leaned away, gazing down at me.

I lifted my chin. "Yes, but it's my last week, so I don't think they'll make me wrap silverware or anything. I should be off no later than nine."

"Excellent." He punctuated this word with another kiss to my forehead, then released me. "I'll pick you up."

"Sounds good." I let him go and picked up my coffee, sighing the sigh of a woman who already misses her guy, even before he's walked out the door.

Too soon, he was gone.

Our time together always felt too short. And the time apart always felt too long.

Clearly, I'd become ridiculous.

Getting ready for the day, I laughed at this strange, new version of myself. And then I laughed at his frustration this morning, though it echoed mine in many ways. Anticipation was all well and good; torture could be sweet, for sure.

Until it wasn't.

Until that simmering thunderstorm he carried around erupted into a hurricane. Or multiple tornadoes touching down all at once. Or a sharknado of destruction, *annihilating the trailer park of my heart!*

I made a face, frowning at my reflection in the bathroom mirror.

My heart wasn't a trailer park. It was more like a national park, but with a sculpture garden of nerdy statues doing the robot. And a library.

Whatever.

The point was, did I want to deal with a Luca Kroft severe weather warning? I knew why *I* hadn't complained about the progression of our sexy times, but why hadn't he? Why was he waiting? Why was he so rigid about it? Or *what* was he waiting for?

Perhaps he worried about me? About my experience level, maybe? Not that he needed to be worried. And he would know if he'd just ask me. My kind of nice might've been the goofy kind, but being goofy-nice didn't mean my past was lacking in sexperience.

Contrary to depictions on TV, nerds do it. A lot. With other humans.

I picked up the book I'd been reading yesterday before Luca had come over, *Fledgling*, by Octavia E. Butler and decided to marinate in this problem while I read. The novel was about a seemingly young woman with amnesia who discovers she is not what (or who) she believes herself to be.

It's an awesome book. I knew this to be true because I'd already read it several times. I especially liked how Butler illuminated self-bias, how the image we see in the mirror can lead us to believe we are one thing, when we are really another thing entirely, and—

Wait a darn minute, Dostoyevsky.

Another thing entirely!

I shot up in my seat, my index finger raised in front of me, suddenly gripped by a thought, or a suspicion, or an idea. Or rather, something like all three.

A "*thopicea*." That's what it was, thought + suspicion + idea = thopicea, the most badass made up word of all time.

So I took my gripping thopicea and I ran to my closet, grinning at both my genius and my leather pants.

** LUCA **

A rare opportunity, a call for abstracts issued by the State Department, on the topic of mutual understanding and cultural context between the United States and Russia, had been sent to me some eleven months ago by an acquaintance of mine at Princeton. He'd stumbled across the RFA while searching the Department of Defense website.

I'd applied for the grant, which had a yearly estimated budget of two million dollars for five years. I'd worked on it tirelessly for three months, fully expecting nothing to come of it other than improved understanding of grantsmanship.

Now, seated in my office, after leaving Anna—her razor wit, thought-provoking conversation, warm bed, and exquisite body—I lost my ability to draw breath for the second time that day.

The award email, wherein the grants manager at the State Department congratulated me and my team, and spelled out next steps—a meeting in Washington, DC, a conference call with our Grants Administration Department, documents needed for the transfer of funds—appeared in my inbox with no fanfare, prosaic in its initial uniformity to any other email.

Yet nothing about this email, or award, or grant, was prosaic. My first thought was to call Anna.

I wanted, more than anything, to share this moment with her. This moment of triumph. This moment of freedom.

But then fear wrestled alongside hope. I struggled to accept the reality and ramifications of this news. Years of living as Sergey Kroft's son meant I had to ask: did my father have connections at the State Department? And could this be one of his maneuverings?

He was powerful, to be sure, but I'd never known him to be capable of this level of corruption. Purchasing and funding an endowed chair at a prestigious university was light years away from rigging the federal grants system.

Even so, I reached for my cell and hurriedly found Dominika's number, counting the rings before she answered.

"Luca?"

"Did he make this happen?"

A pause, and then, "What are we talking about?"

"Dad."

"Did he make what happen?"

"You know what."

Another pause, and then, "Are we talking about the gala? Because that's not set in stone, and you would only have to show up for an hour or two."

I wasn't aware of any gala, nor would I refuse to attend an event if it were important to my family. "Not the gala, Dominika. The grant."

"The grant?"

"Yes. The State Department grant." My heart beating out of my chest, I waited for her answer, the sense that my very life, my entire future hung in the balance did not feel like an overly dramatic estimation.

"Holy crap, are you saying you got the grant?"

"Did he do it?"

"What? No! No, why would he? Oh my God, you got it?"

A gush of air left my lungs and I sunk further into my chair, not prepared to entirely trust my good fortune. "Are you sure?"

"Yes. Yes, I'm sure. There's no way." She lowered her voice to just above a whisper, "There's no way he'd be responsible, even partially. He's anxious for you to leave teaching, take more responsibility and interest in the family business. A grant like this will cement your career and give you the freedom to go anywhere. He'd never do this. You know he's just waiting for you to—"

"Move past my rebellious phase," I finished for her, truth finally penetrating doubt.

"Congratulations, little brother." Dominika was smiling, I heard it in her voice. "I'm proud of you."

Her words of praise hit me square in the chest, my throat constricting, but I managed, "Thank you."

"What are you going to do? Will you stay there? Or take the grant and run?"

I sought out my computer screen, skimming the words of the email again. Reading it this time and in no doubt of its veracity, I had no idea whether I would stay or leave my position.

But I did know exactly how—and with whom—I would spend my evening.

No more waiting, no more restraint. No more cause for caution. The shackles had fallen off, the burden of uncertainty had been lifted. My life was now my own and I was free to give it, and share it, and live it with whomever I chose.

I hadn't yet determined how best to answer my sister's inquiry when the sound of someone opening my office door fractured my attention.

I glanced up from the email and found her hovering in the doorway.

Anna.

"So, how are you?" The cadence of her voice was smooth, deeper than usual, and the way she said the words made them sound rehearsed.

I immediately hung up on my sister, tapping the red *end call* button. She wouldn't like that, and I'd need to apologize later. But for now, I took the extra precaution of turning my cell completely off. I wanted no interruptions, the moment was too momentous.

"Anna." I stood, intent on gathering her to me and indulging in the perfect feel of her.

But the mischievous glint in her eye and slant to her smile halted my would-be progress. She gripped a large raincoat closed at her chest. The rest of her, the black lining her eyes and the red paint of her lips, the high heels she wore, gradually materialized for me as she shut the door.

She locked it.

I lifted an eyebrow at her coat. Summer had not yet relinquished its mild breeze to its chillier successor, fall. Nor was it raining.

"I do like the way you say my name." Her grin widened as she added, "Professor Kroft."

She gave the impression of one who had arrived with purpose. Anna was up to something.

"I'm not your professor." Allowing myself to wonder as my stare wandered over the bulky outer layer, my attention dawdled where the coat ended just below her ankles.

Recollections, searing flashes of memory, of Anna this morning, exposed and panting on her bed, assaulted me with wounding force.

Equally overwhelming, the realization that every barrier

between us had now been conquered. I'd spent the last month rushing to complete my novel and applying for every grant— no matter how large or small, or aligned to my research area and interests—determined to be deserving of her greatness.

Looking upon her now I realized I would never be deserving of her greatness, her kindness and cleverness and joy. My waiting had been in vain. How does one hope to deserve a star? Or hold it? Or keep it?

You don't.

The answer is to always seek. To forever strive. To take and cherish when brilliance is offered.

"That's right, you're not my professor." Anna tilted her head as though deliberating my statement, unbuttoning the top button of her coat. "So I guess that explains why we're allowed to kiss so much."

"Mmm." I decided I would take her to dinner. Tonight. Someplace private, quiet. We would celebrate our freedom.

And then I would seduce her.

And I would keep her in bed for several days, attending to her every need. And whims. If Andrei had but seized his chance with Natasha, he might've lived a long, happy life, mired in deep, thorough satisfaction.

Anna unfastened the second and third button, crossing to me with measured steps. "But that doesn't explain why we haven't done much of anything *other than* kiss. So, why is that, professor?"

I didn't answer, a sensible explanation caught in my throat as she opened the coat, revealing a familiar purple top and her leather pants.

The leather pants.

My mouth watered.

She tossed the coat to the couch. "This is the same outfit I wore when we first met, except—"

I remembered the first time I saw her, how she'd filled these pants, how they'd highlighted every sensual dip and curve. How difficult it had been to concentrate on her words when faced with the glow of her warm, tawny skin, the enticing swell of her breasts, the joyfulness of her smile, the lush fullness of her lips.

"I remember." Unthinkingly, I rushed forward to intercept her.

Anna chuckled, evading my touch by stepping to the side and lifting a finger between us. "Wait, don't you want to know what's different?"

"You can't run away?" I followed, stalking her as she walked backward to avoid me, skirting my desk.

"No." She seemed disconcerted—perhaps by my words, or maybe by the look in my eye as I chased her around my desk—nevertheless, she grinned. "My underwear is different." She reached for the zipper at the front of her pants. "You had no idea last time, but I was wearing my regular old cotton undies. But not this time. This time I'm wearing teeny tiny lace panties and a matching bra." She showed off a purple scrap of lace at her hip.

My flare of impatience was tempered only marginally by the happy, teasing light of her eyes. Anna was still walking backwards, but had nearly expired her options. With no place left to go, her back connected with the door and she was forced to stop.

"So, my point is," she continued evenly, conversationally, "You can't ever really tell about a person, just by looking at them. And sometimes that 'not knowing' even extends to yourself, based on what you see in the mirror, what your interests are, how you-you-you dress yourself, for example." She swallowed the last word, stumbling over her sentence as I invaded her space.

Placing my hands flat against the door on either side of her, caging her in, I brushed a light kiss against her lips.

Perhaps I wouldn't wait.

Perhaps I would take her now.

In my office.

In her leather pants.

Or rather, out of them.

"Luca, are you listening?" Her large eyes were alert and I leaned just slightly away, my stare lowering to her chest. "You don't know unless you ask, right? Sometimes you have to peel back layers—even within yourself—to get to the teeny tiny underwear, as an example. Do you understand what I'm trying to—oh!"

While she spoke, I'd lowered my lips to her neck, tugged her top and bra strap to one side, and bit her shoulder. She lifted her hands, her fingers dug into my scalp, holding me in place.

"Do you know what I wanted to do?" Pulling the top and bra more forcefully to reveal an extravagance of skin, I kissed her again. "When you came here the first time, telling me I gave you nothing."

"No. What? What did you want?" Her breath hitched. It was a blissful sound, a surrender and an invitation as her body arched forward, connecting with mine.

Pulling her to me while also crushing her against the door, much like I'd done the first time we'd kissed, I let her feel what I'd wanted, what I wanted now.

Her breath hitched again.

"Oh. Okay. Well, we should do something about that." Frantically, she yanked at my shirt.

My thumbs pushed into her unzipped leather pants and teeny tiny underwear, sliding the pair down and off as she efficiently kicked away her shoes.

"So we're doing this now?" Anna sounded out of breath.

I captured her wrists as she tried to force my shirt upward and brought them over her head, claiming her lips with a quelling kiss, reminiscent of our first. Transferring both of her hands to one of mine, I reached between her shoulder blades and unclasped her bra, elevating the shirt and sliding my hands beneath, massaging and savoring the full, luscious weight of her in my palm.

She dragged her mouth from mine, twisting her head to the side but holding my gaze, her breathing heavy and excited. "If I'd known all I had to do was wear my leather pants . . ."

I leaned away and absorbed the sight of her, mussed and undone. Her leather pants and lace underwear gone, her hands trapped above her head, the teasing yet seductive tilt of her chin.

Gone were thoughts of caution and propriety, leaving only my insatiability for this captivating woman and her desires.

I released her wrists and removed her top, because I needed her completely bare. I captured her mouth and lifted her, carrying her to my desk. With determined movements, she pulled once more at my shirt, lifting it off and away. Her hands were grasping, reaching for me with purpose.

"See now," she moaned, kissing my chest and trailing her fingertips over my stomach to my belt buckle, "you're just unfair. Must you be so beautiful?"

I covered her hands, stilling her progress and drawing her eyes to mine. "Lie back."

"Luca—"

"Lie back," I guided her to the surface of the desk and unfastened my belt and fly, memorizing the sight of her, as she was now.

Wide, watchful kaleidoscopic eyes; a hint of vulnerability; lush mouth, parted, though she pulled her full bottom lip through her teeth, revealing her uncertainty; her rich, dark tawny skin was a river of silk and velvet; and her hands gripped the edge of the desk as though to brace herself.

Spectacular.

Beyond the feeble capacity of words.

Defying the banality of description.

I stepped between her knees, spreading her wide, bending to brush a feathering kiss along her jaw and the graceful length of her neck. Her hands came to my back, her nails scratching lightly between my shoulder blades as I kissed a wet trail down her body, savoring each delectable inch.

"Oh God, oh God." Anna panted, releasing me, her hands moving to grip the desk above her even as she lifted her head to watch my progress.

A groan escaped my chest as I finally, *finally* tasted her. I'd waited too long to repeat this magnificent act, and now I couldn't remember why. I'd been circumspect and controlled where I should have been deferential. Her body and soul were deserving of worship, never neglect.

Never again.

"Luca!"

"Mmm."

She reached for me, grasping. "Please. Oh, please. I want you. Please, please, please."

I kissed the inside of her thigh and she shuddered, her hands frantic now, searching. Lifting her knees until her heels rested on the edge of the desk, I stroked her with my thumb, circling her silken center as I entered her and she yielded to me.

This time when she shuddered, I did as well, the dazzling truth of her body devastating, as all-consuming as she was stunning, stretched out before me, open, bare, bathed in yearning and trust. She glowed with it, all resplendent beauty and surrendering softness.

Our eyes locked, her hands continued searching for purchase, her mouth working to no purpose, parting with gasping breaths. Threading our fingers together, I bent to her, sliding my tongue against hers, mating our mouths in rhythm to our bodies.

I thought I'd been insatiable for her before, but now I knew there would never be an end to it, my appetite for her moans and sighs, or the hot perfection of her body.

"I'm going to- I'm going to—"

Increasing tempo, I succumbed to a most necessary roughness, to which she responded with high pitched murmurings and whimpers of encouragement, her body bowing to mine as she endured my coarse, pounding intrusion.

"Oh, Luca. Yes, yessss—"

I silenced her cries with a kiss meant to brand, racing towards my own crisis, craving the taste of her on my tongue as I swallowed her moans of gratification. Her once pliant body tensed, pulsing, sending stars into my vision.

And I followed her, my Natasha, my dearest Anna, into shared bliss.

* * *

She wore my shirt and nothing else while we lounged on my couch, her head on my chest, her hand over my heart.

And I knew, very soon, she'd want a shower. The thought brought a smile to my lips.

But for now, Anna was quiet, contemplative. Meanwhile, I wanted her again. Plans swirled, strategies, campaigns and schemes. Soon, we would be in my bed and I wouldn't let her leave until her voice was hoarse, her body boneless, and her desires thoroughly satiated.

Even then, I would keep her close. I would shield her from cruelty, if she'd allow it. And I'd attend to her happiness so long as my doing so contributed to her pleasure.

"What are you thinking about?" Anna lifted her head, propping her chin with the base of her palm.

"How much I want you." I pushed her curls over her shoulder, enjoying the texture of the mahogany spirals.

"You just had me, Andrei." Anna grinned, her gaze cherishing.

"You must know, Andrei will never be satisfied. He will always want more of her. He will forever be wanting to steal her moments and keep her within arm's reach. Thus is the nature of Andrei's insatiable hunger for his Natasha."

She wrinkled her nose, glaring at me with mock suspicion. "Are you saying I can't satisfy my man?"

I laughed at her tart reply, sliding my hand along her spine to massage and stroke her wonderfully bare bottom.

Her expression cleared, sobered as she snuggled closer, and her voice was so quiet, I saw her mouth form the words rather than heard the sound of them. "Luca, I love you."

I started, my whole world expanding and contracting in a single instant. Gathering her close, I shifted to my side such that we were facing each other and I kissed her. I kissed her with all the passion and wonder I felt for this remarkable person who'd chosen me.

Unable to keep my lips from her skin, I bequeathed a necklace of kisses to her neck, gripping her body, this body I loved, and had loved. I couldn't bear the thought of letting her go.

"Luca?" Fingers twisted in my hair, her voice uncertain.

"I love you, Anna. I love you. I love you."

She smiled a joyful smile, though her eyes narrowed. "Even though I'm not your kind of nice?"

"What?" Her words confused me—especially in that moment—as they made no sense, and Anna always made sense.

"Even though you're a world expert on all the impressive things, and I'm just plain Anna?"

Not knowing how to respond to such a ridiculous estimation of her person, I dismissed it. "Your statement is preposterous. Kiss me."

Her grin remained, even as I recaptured her lips, her palms cradling my face. We kissed until air became a concern, and then I reluctantly bent my head to her neck and breathed her in, her hands now rubbing small circles over my back.

"Well," she sighed, sounding content. "This has been a very efficacious day."

"It's not over yet."

"Ah, yes." I felt the grin in her words. "What should we eat? Other than each other, I mean?"

Again, she made me laugh. And this time, she laughed too.

* * *

"If we are not taught how to love, or that we should, then how can we love ourselves? It would be like expecting an infant to fry an egg."

"Luca."

"Anna." I held the door open for her to Jake Peterson's Microbrewery and she preceded me, administering a wane look as she passed.

But I had a point.

Her statement earlier, that she was not my kind of nice, beleaguered and nagged. She'd said it before, when we were in my family's penthouse, after I'd submitted to my weakness, my need to see her, and tracked Anna down at her work.

'I'm not your kind of nice,' she'd said. The words hadn't merited my attention, a throw-away line, I'd believed at the time.

But now, after hearing them from her exquisite mouth a second time, I was not so sure.

"You can't be serious." Anna turned to the hostess and signaled that we required a table for two.

I murmured, "As a blood infection," so only she could hear.

"Come on." She shook her head, but was thwarted in her rebuttal as the hostess motioned for us to follow her into the restaurant.

However, as soon as we were seated side-by-side in our booth and the hostess had left us to examine the menu, Anna leaned toward me, placing her hand on my arm. "Come on. You can't look for completion with another person. You have to know yourself first."

"Yes, I agree. Know thyself. But love thyself? No."

"You don't love yourself?"

"I didn't say that. I merely argue that this postmodern individualism is harmful, that we—Western society—have become lazy in our dependencies and relationships. To say, 'Don't attempt to love another until you know what it is to love yourself,' is imbecilic. We, humans, must be loved *first* to know how to love in return. This is why we are given families, ideally parents, who will love us, teach us that we are worthwhile, worthy of love and respect, provide a mirror, a reflection of our worth. We must know what love is, what it looks like, in order to give it to another."

"I don't think that's true." She crossed her arms, glaring at me. "And furthermore, I think I want a hamburger and a milkshake."

I closed my menu. "I'll have what you're having, even though you're wrong."

She rolled her eyes, glancing heavenward. "How can you think this way?"

"Think of love, an accurate representation of yourself, like an egg. You've never seen an egg, never had it cooked for you, never cooked it yourself, never eaten it. Then, suddenly, I give you an egg and ask you to make me an omelet. According to your perspective, you are not allowed to touch the egg until you know how to cook it. But then, how will you learn?"

"*I* can touch the egg, I just can't cook it for *you*. I would have to cook it for myself first. Read about it, take some cooking lessons. Maybe visit a chicken farm."

"Really? We would put everything on hold—after finding each other, after navigating the magnificent messiness of our journey thus far—so you could take some time to become more self-sufficient?"

"What's wrong with being self-sufficient?"

"What's wrong with being vulnerable? With trusting another person to see *who* you are and love you for it."

Her eyes narrowed into an imitation of a glare, but her mouth twisted to the side to hide a smile.

I leaned closer, indulging the urge to trace the line of her jaw with my fingertip, then a gentle glide to the base of her neck where her pulse quickened beneath her skin.

"I do not wish for a companion," my attention was drawn to her remarkable lips, "for an alluring fish from the sea, one of many self-sufficient salmon." I lifted my stare to hers, finding amusement illuminating her eyes. "Or halibut."

"Are you calling me a halibut? Because I've always considered myself more of a largemouth bass."

I laughed, keeping my thumb against her pulse point and draping my fingers along her neck and shoulder, "No. You are no fish, nor am I."

"Then what are you saying?"

I brushed a light kiss against her temple, whispering, "Come as you are, Anna."

I felt the hesitation in her, the contradiction on the tip of her tongue.

"Come self-sufficient. Come powerful. Or come weak and uncertain. Just come to me. And stay. Trust that you are precisely the right piece, because you are the missing piece— in my life and of my heart."

"Oh, Luca." She melted. Her hands grabbed fistfuls of my shirt as her side came in full contact with my chest. She leaned against me and she sighed. "You say the most wonderful things, even if you can't math."

At this I chuckled, lifting her chin with my fingers and rationing just one kiss before forcing her to meet my gaze.

"You are flawless to me." I held her with might and purpose, needing her to feel the veracity of my words. "We fit together like custom pieces from a two person puzzle. And therefore, you are exactly *my* perfect kind of nice."

THE END

Pre-order Penny Reid's next release Marriage of Inconvenience coming 2018!

Read on for a sneak peek of Penny Reid's latest work!

There are three things you need to know about Kat Tanner (aka Kathleen Tyson. . . and yes, she is *that* Kathleen

Tyson): 1) She's determined to make good decisions, 2) She must get married ASAP, and 3) She knows how to knit.

Being a billionaire heiress isn't all it's cracked up to be. In fact, it sucks. Determined to live a quiet life, Kat Tanner changed her identity years ago and eschewed her family's legacy. But now, Kat's silver spoon past has finally caught up with her, and so have her youthful mistakes. To avoid imminent disaster, she must marry immediately; it is essential that the person she chooses have no romantic feelings for her whatsoever and be completely trustworthy.

Fortunately, she knows exactly who to ask. Dan O'Malley checks all the boxes: single, romantically indifferent to her, completely trustworthy. Sure, she might have a wee little crush on Dan the Security Man, but with clear rules, expectations, and a legally binding contract, Kat is certain she can make it through this debacle with her sanity—and heart—all in one piece.

Except, what happens when Dan O'Malley isn't as indifferent—or as trustworthy—as she thought?

Marriage of Inconvenience is book #7 in the *Knitting in the City* series and is **available for pre-order now!**

ABOUT THE AUTHOR

Penny Reid lives in Seattle, Washington with her husband, three kids, and an inordinate amount of yarn. She used to spend her days writing federal grant proposals as a biomedical researcher, but now she just writes books.

Come find me-
Mailing list signup: http://pennyreid.ninja/newsletter/ (get exclusive stories, sneak peeks, and pictures of cats knitting hats)
Facebook: http://www.facebook.com/PennyReidWriter
Instagram: https://www.instagram.com/reidromance/
Goodreads: http://www.goodreads.com/ReidRomance
Email: pennreid@gmail.com ...hey, you! Email me ;-)
Blog: http://pennyreid.ninja
Twitter: https://twitter.com/ReidRomance
Ravelry: http://www.ravelry.com/people/ReidRomance (if you crochet or knit...!)

Please, write a review!
If you liked this book (and, more importantly perhaps, if you didn't like it) please take a moment to post a review some-place (Amazon, Goodreads, your blog, on a bathroom stall wall, in a letter to your mother, etc.). It helps society more than you know when you make your voice heard; reviews force us to move towards a true meritocracy.

SNEAK PEEK: NOBODY LOOKS GOOD NAKED

A PENNY REID NEWSLETTER
EXCLUSIVE: SUBSCRIBE NOW!

*P*rofessor Hanover's eyes were affixed to his smartphone with the determined unsteadiness of a man who was exceedingly uncomfortable.

Meanwhile, I was in the precarious position of being naked.

Wait. Let me back up a second and explain. Most people aren't aware that there are five stages of naked.

The first, and most obvious of course, is just buck-bare-naked. No clothes, no nothing. All skin.

The second stage is virtually naked. The nipples might be covered with a bit of sequence, but not always. Typically all that is needed is a strategically placed triangle secured to the front lady parts by either adhesive or barely visible plastic string. Usually the bottom is completely exposed.

Stage number three is almost naked. The boob—the nipple at a minimum—is scarcely veiled and panties of some kind are worn, frequently a G-string or floss-like thong.

Stage four is still a type of naked, but some would argue it may also venture into the not-technically-naked category. We call it transparently naked and it normally involves a bra, panties, or lingerie of some sort. However—whatever the items—they are completely see through, sheer lace. As such, very little is obstructing the eye from the skin beneath.

Finally, stage five just manages to cross the line from naked to not naked. It is being in a state of undress, donning conservative underthings—like an opaque nightie, or a long slip—and is commonly referred to as disrobed.

But back to me being naked in front of my professor.

I hadn't recognized him at first. I don't look at the faces of clients. I exit the session with a vague impression of a person like, 'that guy who smelled like peanuts' or, 'the really tall one who tried to touch my boob.'

They, the men and sometimes their second wives or mistresses, were always looking at my body, never my face or eyes. So looking directly at the customers seemed unnecessary.

Actually, let me amend that, they weren't looking at me. They were looking at what I was wearing. At first, when I started, I assumed they were assessing whether seven hundred dollars was too much to pay for a bra. But the longer I worked for The Pinkery as a lingerie model, the more I began to understand that the clients weren't concerned with money. They had plenty of money.

They were concerned with their own boredom.

Which meant I only ever noticed someone, really saw them, if they weren't looking at me.

Victor Hanover – Dr. Hanover, my Research Methods professor – wasn't looking at me.

He was looking at his phone.

Thank God.

Because I was currently stage three naked.

"Hello…?"

I blinked against the murkiness of mortified recognition and turned my attention to the only other person in the room. He was older than Dr. Hanover, nicely dressed, with silver hair at his temples. The unknown man was also smaller than my professor, but somehow his presence felt larger, suffocating.

I couldn't focus on this older man's face, but not for the usual reasons. I was distracted, too busy arbitrating the wrestling match between my shock and embarrassment. Embarrassment was winning.

"I said, could you turn?" he snapped.

I nodded, turned, happy to show them my basically bare backside if it gave me a moment to collect myself.

Dr. Hanover and this older man were sitting in a private room—my private room—at The Pinkery. As the most exclusive lingerie, fripperies, and accoutrements shop in New England, it required a membership and minimum monthly purchase guarantee for entry and continued access. I wasn't used to seeing anyone I knew in real life while at work. Neither my classmates nor my professors could afford the membership or the merchandise.

For that matter, the scraps of lace and silk were firmly out of my budget as well.

"What do you think, Victor?"

I swallowed, being careful to do so quietly. The last thing I wanted was to be the source of a cartoonish gulp while my professor contemplated my ass. He was looking at my ass. I was sure of it. I knew the precise moment his eyes lifted to my skin and I gritted my teeth, feeling the affliction of his gaze traveling lower, over my thighs.

Call it a sixth sense, call it intuition, but I always knew where the clients were looking. This uncanny ability usually came in handy as it meant I could focus my energy on highlighting that area, giving it the best light, angling my leg just-so.

But not this time. This time I held perfectly still like I used to do when caught by my mother with my hand in the cookie jar. And by cookie jar, I mean my hand in my high school boyfriend's pants, in the back of my car on prom night.

My mother—God love her—tossed three condoms into the backseat and called over her shoulder, "You better get my daughter off before you come all over her car."

I hadn't inherited my mother's impressive talent for punchline delivery, but I had inherited her pragmatic nature. I'd always been more likely to freeze than flee, or fight, or flirt when faced with a mortifying situation.

Which was why I stood stock still as I heard Professor Hanover clear his throat before saying, "I'm not sure where I should be looking."

"Oh for God's sake," the older man huffed with obvious impatience, "The model, Victor. Look at the model."

"Why? She's not for sale."

I closed my eyes, pressing my lips together. It was such a Dr. Hanover thing to say, much more in character than glaring uncomfortably at the screen of his smartphone.

Over the last two months of sitting through his course, I'd never once seen him uncomfortable, though I'd seen him glare plenty. Glare at students who took too long to answer. Glare at students who were obviously unprepared for class. Glare at students who couldn't quite grasp the concept of a split tailed T-test.

He glared all the time, in that exasperated 'I'm so much smarter than you, you might as well be a single-celled organism in comparison' kind of way.

But uncomfortable? Never.

It was Victor's turn to sigh. "I don't know why you brought me."

The older man made a sniffing sound. "Is it so odd that I would want to spend time with my son?"

His. . . son? What? Wait. That's weird, right? Who would take their son to a lingerie shop? Or maybe this practice was all the rage and I was completely out of touch.

Victor scoffed, and I imagined he was rolling his eyes. I'd never seen him roll his eyes, he was far too enlightened for that, but—for some reason—I imagined him as rolling his eyes now.

"Fine. Lyla suggested it." The older man lowered his voice to a gruff whisper.

"Who's Lyla?"

"Victor . . ." the single word was ripe with warning.

"I'm sorry, is she one of your wives? I've lost count, so you can't expect me to remember names."

Now I rolled my lips between my teeth, because that was also a very Professor Hanover thing to say. The man was firmly in the asshole column, but his sarcastic sass always made me laugh (sometimes against my will). This meant I was frequently ducking my head and hiding behind my laptop during class.

It also meant that I never, ever, ever put myself in the position of being on the receiving end of his sarcasm. I knew the Research Methods textbooks so well, I probably could've taught the course at this point.

But back to the good professor and his mad dad.

"Don't I deserve happiness?" the older man ranted, "Don't I—"

Victor made another scoffing sound, raising his voice over his father's. "You want to keep looking for happiness between a woman's legs? Fine. Go for it. But don't fucking bring me here and expect father-son bonding time. Sitting in a bourgeois lingerie store, slobbering over a woman one third your age while your current wife—"

"You know we're engaged," his father thundered, and it sounded like he'd lunged to his feet.

"Whatever," Victor's voice also rose, "Current vagina of the moment—"

Whoa!

"Mr. Hanover," a woman's voice cut in, silencing both men.

But not just any woman's voice. Madame Purple, my boss, and a take-no-bullshit-or-prisoners kind of super woman. She reported directly to the owner, Madame Pink.

At the sound of her voice I flinched, half turning on instinct. But then I stopped myself and offered just my profile. From my vantage point I could see the professor, standing, facing his father. Unable to help myself I looked at him; I'd been so shocked by his presence earlier, I hadn't taken a moment to study the man.

Firstly, he looked pissed, his eyes flashing fire, his hands clenched into fists.

Secondly, I realized he wasn't in his usual baggy dad-jeans and dorktastic, overly large, brown and yellow striped button down shirt. With a pocket protector.

One shirttail tucked in, one shirttail flapping in the breeze. No. Not today.

Today he was wearing a dark blue tailored suit. And it fit. And he looked damn fine in it. It made him seem taller. . . or was it the waves of menace and fury? Or had he always been tall?

Also, I'd never witnessed his hair anything other than flat and ignored. Not today. His hair was styled as though the man knew how to style it. However, he did don his usual black horned-rimmed glasses. The effect of this makeover plus the glasses gave Victor Hanover a distinctly nerdy-sexy-Calvin Klein-model vibe that. . . well, it startled me.

He was still firmly in the asshole column, but now he was in the sexy asshole column.

"What?" Victor's dad didn't try to veil his impatience with my boss's interruption.

She smiled at the two men, her purple, shimmery lipstick a gorgeous complement to her velvety, brown skin. "You have a phone call."

"What?"

"A phone call."

Mr. Hanover straightened, his gaze flickering over her like he couldn't decide whether to be indignant or furious.

But before he could question Madame Purple further, she volunteered, "It's Madame Pink. She wishes to discuss the status of your membership."

Oh. Snap.

My eyes widened, but I caught the crack in my demeanor almost instantly. Schooling my expression, I gathered a silent breath.

There was no three-strikes and you're out policy at The Pinkery. You were out when Madame Pink said you were out. End of story. She never explained why. And once you were out, you could never get back in.

Mr. Hanover shifted restlessly on his feet. "I apologize if our raised voices caused any disturbance." It looked like the words poisoned him as he spoke them. I imagined this man rarely—if ever—apologized. This suspicion was confirmed as his son glanced between Madame Purple and his father, seemingly confused, or astonished, or both.

"Please," Madame Purple widened her smile, stepping to

one side and motioning to the door with a graceful movement of her hand, "After you."

Mr. Hanover slid his teeth to the side and sent his son a quick, incensed look. Then the man turned a rigid grin to my boss and gave her a little head nod, strolling unhurriedly out of the room while fiddling with his cuff-links.

My boss gave Professor Hanover a whisper of a smile, then to me indicated with her chin toward the bar console in the corner. "Lavender, please pour a glass of scotch for your guest. And . . ." Her eyes moved back to him and she studied his openly bewildered expression for several beats before continuing, "And perhaps the black and red garter ensemble next."

I wanted to wince. I wanted to wince so hard. Or at the very least communicate my panic with a glance of extreme askance. It would be the most askance glance in the history of glances.

But I didn't. Mostly because I was frozen. But also because Madame Purple didn't give me chance. She turned on her heel and left.

Oh jeez.

Well.

Okay then.

Here I go.

. . . I couldn't move.

But I had to move. I glanced at the camera, artfully hidden in the corner, and reminded myself of how much I wanted this job—for the record, it was a lot.

Finally, I did it. I forced my feet to carry me towards the bar.

"Where are you going?" Professor Hanover's voice was heavily seasoned with suspicion; my steps faltered at his tone.

I didn't stop, though my gaze instinctively lifted and

connect with his, causing my chest to tighten with dread. I ignored the sensation. Instead I focused on his frown. To my immense relief, I saw his gaze was cloudy with something like frustration, but definitely not recognition.

I motioned to the bar and continued towards it, saying nothing. If I could help it, I rarely spoke in front of clients, just what was required according to our guidelines. But beyond that, I wondered if Dr. Hanover was more likely to recognize my voice than my face.

I was quiet in class, answering succinctly whenever he called my name. And I typically wore a hat with my hair tucked up inside or pulled back in a ponytail. I also never wore makeup outside of work, mostly because makeup was expensive. In addition to inheriting my mother's pragmatism, I'd also inherited her frugal nature.

Flexing my fingers, I relaxed, realizing that the chances of him recognizing me were actually fairly low. He had, what? Over a hundred students in that lecture hall every week? And that was just my class.

Slowly, I placed my hands on the glassware, pleased to see they weren't shaking. I'd just removed the stopper to the decanter and released a steady breath when he spoke again.

"I'm sorry."

My fingers stilled and I glanced at him, discovering that my professor was strolling towards me. His hands in his pants pockets, his attention on the bar console. He stopped a few feet away while I tried to stand as nonchalantly as possible.

Have you ever tried to stand nonchalantly before? Like tried to be pointedly disinterested? Or "act normal?" It's impossible. It's like trying to pee on a target with an audience of five hundred nuns.

Not to mention, Victor Hanover had just apologized. To me. For I had no idea what.

The mere idea of the superior professor apologizing to anyone for anything had me questioning whether I was awake, or if this was a dream, or maybe I was high. Granted, I'd never touched drugs. Nevertheless, the possibility of being high felt more likely than Dr. Hanover apologizing.

"I'm sorry," he repeated, his voice softer, his gaze resting everywhere but on me, "My words were sarcastic and spoken in anger. They were meant to reflect how my father views women, and are not indicative of my own thoughts. He is a faithless taint, and should be despised. For the record, I do not share his . . ." Victor's eyes moved to the left, as though he were searching for the right words. "I do not share his lack of respect for other humans, especially female humans. Therefore, I'm sorry you heard it. But more than that, I'm sorry I said it."

Well... huh.

How about that.

Unable to tear my gaze away, I stared at him, openly examining my professor. His eyes were a dark color—maybe dark green, maybe brown—it was hard to see them behind his glasses. His nose reminded me of Brad Pitt's nose; smaller than the average man-nose, but strangely it worked for him. Victor's jaw was angular, strong, and covered in late after-noon scruff. He was probably one of those guys who had to shave twice a day.

Victor Hanover was so. . . odd.

And quite suddenly made enormously attractive by his apology.

This abrupt discovery of his attractiveness—especially relative to his previous plainness and firm placement in the asshole column—overwhelmed me.

Maybe because I'd never been this close to him? Maybe because I'd never seen him impassioned? Maybe because I'd never seen him as anything other than a dry, distracted, and aloof goof? Or maybe because I'd never looked at Professor Hanover before and thought of him as a man.

As brilliant? Yes. As funny and witty? Yes and yes. As a sadist who enjoyed torturing his students and forcing them to learn all relevant applications of the chi-square test? Yes, yes, and yes.

But never as a man.

It was overwhelming. He was overwhelming. The crush alarm sounded between my ears and low in my stomach. My face flushed with heat and I swallowed a breath.

Ahhhhh crap.

He was still staring beyond me, lost in his own thoughts, which gave me a precious moment to compose myself. I needed it.

This wasn't good. I still had two months in this man's class and he called on every student at least once a week. He might not ever recognize me, but crushes made me tongue tied and stupid. If I were tongue-tied and stupid for this man, he'd squash me like an ant.

Plus—hello—I was standing in the same room as him, stage three naked, lest I forget.

"What's your name?" He still hadn't looked directly at me.

"Lavender," I answered breathlessly without thinking. Had his voice always been so deliciously deep?

"No. What's your real name?"

I shook my head, my mouth forming a tight smile as I glanced quickly at the camera in the corner, then busied myself with making his drink.

He followed my gaze, then whispered, "We're being watched?"

I nodded, my smile growing a smidge more sincere as I

held out the glass of liquor I'd just poured. After a short moment of hesitation, he accepted the glass, his fingers brushing against mine. A shiver raced own my spine at the contact but I ignored it, stepping, turning, and strolling away toward the open rack of lingerie.

Going through the motions, I decided I'd put the garter ensemble—which consisted of a red and black bone-bustier with garter straps and thigh-high silk stockings—over the bra and thong I was already wearing.

I'd just finished rolling up the second stocking when he said, "You don't have to do that."

Looking to him, I lifted a questioning eyebrow. He'd stayed by the bar, one hand in his pocket, the other holding his drink. His posture was relaxed as he took another swallow of scotch, but he'd yet to meet my gaze.

"Do what?"

"Don't you have a robe?"

I straightened. "Do you want to see a robe?"

"Wouldn't you be more comfortable? If you were less . . ." He scratched the back of his neck, his attention on the wall behind me.

"Less?"

"If you were covered?"

I blinked at him and answered before I could think better of my response. "No. Would you?"

"You wouldn't?" Once again, he was strolling toward me, this time his gaze was on his drink. "It doesn't bother you? Being objectified?"

"Think of me as a clothes hanger." That's mostly how I thought about it.

He snorted, his features twisting with amusement and disbelief. "My imagination isn't that good," he said to his scotch.

"Fine. Then a mannequin."

Dr. Hanover's eyes flickered quickly over my form and he appeared to stand straighter, the muscle at his jaw jumping as he ground out, "My imagination isn't that good either."

Sensing his discomfort, I reached for a red, silk kimono and slipped it over my shoulders. "If you'd like to see a robe, I'll wear a robe."

"Do you get paid if you put on the robe?"

"Yes."

"But you don't like the robe?" His inquisitive stare was pointed at my forehead.

"It's a lovely robe." I deflected smoothly, but then stumbled over the next part, "W-would you like to touch it?"

Gah and drat. I had to ask.

Every time we put on a new layer we were supposed to ask the client if they wanted to touch the item. And that meant he could basically touch me anywhere as I was covered from neck to ankle in red silk kimono.

Dr. Hanover drew in a slow breath, his gaze coming to my body, moving lower and lingering this time, as though now that I was no longer naked, he'd given himself permission to actually look at me. His stare moved slowly, caressing a path to my neck, jaw, to my hair where it rested over one shoulder.

Suddenly, his frown returned, and this time he looked thoughtful. He blinked.

And then his eyes shot to mine, growing at once cold and hot, and dread unfurled like a slithery beast in my belly.

He recognized me.

Or rather, he realized he knew me from somewhere, but hadn't quite figured out who I was. Which meant I had exactly two seconds to do something drastic.

Instead—big surprise—I froze.

"Wait a second." Dr. Hanover drew closer, until less than

two feet separated us. Peripherally, on autopilot, I realized I could smell his cologne. He smelled great and I chastised myself for noticing that he smelled great. Especially now. I needed to act, and instead I was sniffing him.

Do something other than smell him!

His eyes were currently flickering over me with urgency, jumping from my breast to my lips to my neck to my eyes. And when they finally settled, I saw that his irises were dark green.

That slithery beast of mortification punched me in the gut as my professor, holding my gaze hostage, whispered, "I know you."

** END SNEAK PEEK **

To read more of *Nobody Looks Good Naked* subscribe to Penny's newsletter where it will be exclusively released monthly beginning in June 2018:
http://pennyreid.ninja/newsletter/

OTHER BOOKS BY PENNY REID

Knitting in the City Series

(Contemporary Romantic Comedy)

Neanderthal Seeks Human: A Smart Romance (#1)

Neanderthal Marries Human: A Smarter Romance (#1.5)

Friends without Benefits: An Unrequited Romance (#2)

Love Hacked: A Reluctant Romance (#3)

Beauty and the Mustache: A Philosophical Romance (#4)

Ninja at First Sight (#4.75)

Happily Ever Ninja: A Married Romance (#5)

Dating-ish: A Humanoid Romance (#6)

Marriage of Inconvenience (#7, coming 2018)

Winston Brothers Series

(Contemporary Romantic Comedy, spinoff of *Beauty and the Mustache*)

Truth or Beard (#1)

Grin and Beard It (#2)

Beard Science (#3)

Beard in Mind (#4)

Dr. Strange Beard (#5, coming 2018)

Beard with Me (#5.5, coming 2019)

Beard Necessities (#6, coming 2019)

Hypothesis Series

(New Adult Romantic Comedy)

Elements of Chemistry: ATTRACTION, HEAT, and
CAPTURE (#1)

Laws of Physics: MOTION, SPACE, and TIME (#2, coming 2018)

Fundamentals of Biology: STRUCTURE, EVOLUTION, and
GROWTH (#3, coming 2019)

Irish Players (Rugby) Series – by L.H. Cosway and Penny Reid

(Contemporary Sports Romance)

The Hooker and the Hermit (#1)

The Pixie and the Player (#2)

The Cad and the Co-ed (#3)